TROUBLE IN Paradise

A Novel by

R B Conroy

CCB Publishing
British Columbia, Canada

Trouble in Paradise

Copyright ©2017 by R B Conroy
ISBN-13 978-1-77143-310-5
First Edition

Library and Archives Canada Cataloguing in Publication
Conroy, R B, 1944-, author
Trouble in paradise / by R B Conroy. -- First edition.
Issued in print and electronic formats.
ISBN 978-1-77143-310-5 (pbk.).--ISBN 978-1-77143-311-2 (pdf)
Additional cataloguing data available from Library and Archives Canada

Cover artwork by Michelle Cline: **www.clinecoversanddesign.com**

Photo image for the cover was provided by photographer Ronnie Clark.

Extreme care has been taken by the author to ensure that all information presented in this book is accurate and up to date at the time of publishing. Neither the author nor the publisher can be held responsible for any errors or omissions. Additionally, neither is any liability assumed for damages resulting from the use of the information contained herein.

Publisher: CCB Publishing
British Columbia, Canada
www.ccbpublishing.com

Acknowledgements

As always, I would like to express my love and gratitude to my lovely wife, Cheryl, for her undying devotion to my writing. Without her considerable efforts, this project would have never been completed. She is without question "The Wind Beneath My Wings."

And although I've never met my amazing publisher, Paul Rabinovitch, after eight books and communications too numerous to count, I feel like he is a friend. In my opinion, CCB Publishing is the best publisher in the business. Thanks again, Paul, for a job well done. I would also like to express my sincere appreciation to our ultra-talented local photographer, Ronnie Clark, who opened his amazing portfolio to me and gave me the wonderful photo that I used on the cover. And many thanks to my fine editor, Suellen Arbuckle, for burning the midnight oil so that I could get this book out on schedule. Thanks so much, Susie!

-It wasn't so much her need for love as it was her desire to share her love with others-

Chapter 1

John Cullen tapped the table several times and gently tossed his fork on the plate next to his half-eaten English muffin. It was noisy inside the busy café and his guest was late arriving. Being a punctual person, he disdained waiting. He looked up as the front door of the tiny café swung open. A giggly teenage girl in jeans and halter top with boyfriend in tow, came bursting in and plopped down at a corner table—another false alarm. His displeasure growing, he lifted the crinkled local rag off the chair next to him and briskly snapped through the pages.

Cullen had worked late the night before at his bank in downtown Tampa so he could enjoy a long weekend at The Villages with his latest squeeze, a thirty something girl named Ali. The Villages is a trendy retirement community near Orlando that consists of over one hundred different neighborhoods or villages and boasts of upwards of fifty golf courses. John had met Ali the previous weekend at Cody's, a popular hangout in The Villages. Near retirement age, John had bought a house in the sprawling retirement community a few years earlier. He likes it there because it is far from his workplace in Tampa, and chockfull of attractive young ladies who work in the many stores and restaurants in the area.

Like most of the girls John picked up, Ali was attractive, non-college educated, financially challenged, and younger than him. John knew from experience that most women like Ali have little in the way of material wealth and were looking for a Sugar Daddy to give them the finer things in life. This made them an easy mark for John and his highly charged sexual appetite. With a million dollar home in the Village of Bridgeport, a large estate in Tampa, and a huge investment portfolio, he had what it took to lure them into bed.

On this morning, his modus operandi had called for a quick breakfast, a dip in his pool, hopefully followed by lengthy sessions of steamy sex in his palatial master bedroom. Afterword, he would dangle the possibility of a long term relationship in front of Ali to insure her availability for future trysts. Then, usually a few weeks or months later, when he felt things were getting a little too cozy in the relationship, he would present her with a delicately crafted good-bye, usually by text or e-mail, and be on his way. After his most recent divorce, a self-absorbed John wanted no part of a long-term commitment.

A glint of light flashed across the restaurant temporarily distracting John from the newspaper. He looked out the restaurant window at the sun reflecting off the windshield of a green Honda Civic. The dilapidated vehicle jerked to a stop in an empty parking spot across from the restaurant. Inside the car, he could see a young lady looking in the rearview mirror and dabbing on lipstick. She quickly exited the car and made her way across the busy street toward the café. John was taken aback by how stunningly attractive she was. *Is it her?* He wasn't certain. He had been extremely drunk the night he met her and it was in the wee hours of the morning. He vaguely remembered them going to his house where he must have passed out, because he couldn't really remember if they made love or not. *I hope we did,* he thought.

He watched with rapt attention as the front door to the restaurant swung open. The leggy beauty eased through the door to the restaurant and quickly surveyed the room. John breathed a quiet sigh of relief—it was her. He remembered she wore a large gold bracelet on her right arm. Dropping the newspaper on the chair next to him, he raised his right hand ever so slightly. She saw the modest gesture and walked quickly toward his table, smiling from ear to ear. As she drew near, he was once again pleasantly surprised by the stark beauty of this woman. Tastefully tight jeans served only to accentuate her long shapely legs. A sequined and very feminine denim vest covered a wispy white cotton blouse. Her light brown hair was pulled back on the sides with several long strands falling haphazardly across her forehead. Her face was a masterpiece of Mother Nature. Light blue eyes and wonderfully proportioned features accentuated by a full and sexy mouth which seemed to invite a kiss from those lucky enough to gaze upon its grandeur. His aggravation over her tardiness was quickly disappearing. His legs felt weak as he stood to greet her.

Still smiling, she extended her hand. "Good morning, John, wonderful to see you again. I'm so sorry I'm late, but my car wouldn't start and my neighbor had to give me a jump. I tried to call you a few times, but your cell went right to voice mail."

"Why....uh no problem. I had a couple of business calls this morning." He tapped the screen on his iPhone, it lit up showing three missed calls. Red crept up his face, "Yes...I see your calls. Please accept my apologies. I must have accidentally turned the ringer off. Sit down, please."

John started to go around the table to pull out her

chair, but to his surprise, she brushed past him and took the seat next to him and scooted a little closer. Shocked by her aggressiveness, John's heart was racing. The striking beauty had him back on his heels. He paused a second to compose himself and then took his seat.

"Would you like some breakfast?" he asked.

"No thanks, I always eat early. I had a bagel at 6:30. But I could use a cup of coffee."

"Certainly." John lifted his cup toward a nearby waitress. She hurried over, pot in hand, and splashed Ali's cup full.

"Thanks, Judy." John smiled at the waitress.

"You're welcome." His friend Judy gave him an approving wink and hurried off.

"How are things at the bank?" Ali asked.

"Oh, okay I guess. We are going through a couple of mergers and they are getting a little tricky. We're buying out two smaller banks and they are reluctant to play by our rules." Ali leaned closer, the wonderful scent of her perfume made John think of the previous weekend—a weekend that took on new meaning as he viewed the seductive creature next to him.

She smiled. "Oh, your job is to take care of mergers?'

"Yes, among other things. I'm the CEO of First Bank of Tampa."

Her brow raised slightly, "CEO?"

"Yes, I'm Chief Executive Officer. In other words,

I'm the boss."

"Of First Bank of Tampa?" Her eyes widened. "How impressive!" He felt a gentle pat on his knee.

John smiled nervously. "So, what would you like to do today? Do you enjoy tennis? Golf? Or would you just like to hang out by my pool and enjoy this warm sunny day?"

"Well, you may not remember, but we talked about going shopping at the mall in Ocala today. I promised a couple of my friends that I would pick a few things up for them. Remember?" She tilted her head charmingly and smiled.

John looked puzzled, he smiled meekly. She was right, John couldn't remember what he said that night. He was so drunk at the time that he could have said anything. But of one thing he was certain—he didn't like her suggestion at all. After the pat to his knee, his fantasies were running wild. He wanted desperately to get her to his place, get that sexy body into a bathing suit, fill her with alcohol, entice her up to his master suite and make mad passionate love to her.

"Are you sure about shopping? It's such a lovely day to spend inside."

He felt another pat on his knee. "I know, but I promised my friends."

"How can I say no to such a pretty face?" John sighed in resignation.

"Should I drive?" she queried.

"Oh no, let's take my car. Anyway, you said you were having car trouble."

"Yes, I am. It's my battery. It's more than five years old and I can't afford to replace it."

"Well, why don't I follow you down to Tire Hut and you can drop your car off and have a new battery installed. We can pick it up when we get back to The Villages and I will have them bill my credit card."

"Oh no, I really don't expect you to...."

"Please, Ali, I insist."

"You're so kind."

"Don't mention it. Shall we go?" John laid a twenty dollar bill on the table, not waiting for the change.

"Yes, I'm ready." She smiled warmly and batted her eyes at the befuddled bank mogul.

Chapter 2

John was feeling a little irritated as he cruised along the winding county road toward I-75. He wasn't accustomed to one of the local party girls setting the agenda for the day. After all, Ali was a woman of little means and he was a big shot banker. He should be deciding how they would spend the day, not her. *Why, the gall of this woman!* His ire was growing.

"You're awfully quiet over there," Ali mused. She turned and moved her crossed legs toward him.

Still aggravated, John tossed a stern glance her way.

"I hope you're not upset about something," she continued.

When his eyes made contact with those beautiful blues, his indignation began to wane. "Why of course not. I've been wanting to get up to the mall in Ocala for some time." John was finding himself unable to sustain any kind of negative feelings toward his seductive aficionado.

John slowed down and veered around a small black pickup that was turning off the highway onto a nearby pathway that led to a large stable of horses.

"Aren't those horses incredibly beautiful?" Ali gazed at several horses grazing in a pasture.

"Yes they are, there are many extraordinary horses in this area. I attend the annual Breeder's Cup near Ocala every year. People come from all over the country to buy young thoroughbreds at the Breeder's Cup. Millions of dollars exchange hands in just a few days. It's a huge event."

"Oh, how interesting!"

John smiled smugly. "We're just about to 75."

"I am so looking forward to spending this day with you."

John forced a weak smile. "Me too, and take your time. I'm in no hurry."

John felt a touch on his forearm. "Oh, thank you."

* * *

About ten minutes later, John exited west off of the interstate toward the mall. When he arrived at the busy mall, he quickly darted in front of another vehicle to grab the only remaining parking spot next to the sidewalk.

Ali grinned broadly, quickly exited the vehicle and started for the sidewalk.

John jumped out the driver's side and shouted, "Wait up!"

He was smiling as he hurried over and grabbed her hand. The two of them quickly merged onto the crowded sidewalk for a day of shopping at the Paddock Mall in Ocala.

* * *

It was late afternoon when the unlikely couple arrived back in The Villages. John drove straight to the repair shop to pick up Ali's car.

Parking directly in front of the glassed-in reception area, he hurried inside to pay her bill. About ten minutes later John returned, slid in the driver's side and handed the car keys to Ali, along with a packet of information.

"Here's the warranty info for your new battery," he explained.

"Oh, thank you so much, John. I really appreciate this and it was so much fun today. I really had a good time."

John grinned broadly. "Why don't you follow me back to my house? We can discuss your undying gratitude over dinner at my place. We'll do steaks on the grill and then enjoy a bottle of my finest Cabernet from my new wine room."

"Oh, I'm so sorry, John, but I can't. I promised my mother that I would have dinner with her this evening. She called this morning and said she had made my favorite chicken casserole. I'm all she has, John, I couldn't let her down. I hope you understand."

John's face flushed red. It seemed to startle Ali. He had been ogling Ali's wonderful legs and shapley backside the entire day just waiting for the chance to get her back to his place. But more importantly, she had changed the agenda once again. A girl like Ali should never say no to a man of his stature. She should forgo a simple evening with her mother when invited to dinner by a man like John Cullen. That was the unspoken rule in John Cullen's world—the rich guy always gets his way. But he also knew that this girl was different—she was no pushover. John forced a smile and quickly tried to compose himself, afraid his disappointment had shown. "Oh...uh, dinner with your mother, chicken casserole. How nice."

Ali studied his face for an instant. Apparently, not happy with his reaction, she was sizing him up. This unnerved John; he broke eye contact and looked away, hoping desperately that his flash of anger had gone unnoticed. He felt like a pathetic child that had fallen in love with the prettiest girl in the class and was trying to win her approval.

Ali cast him a skeptical eye, "Are you sure you're okay with this? For a moment there your face got red.

I could swear you were angry with me."

"Oh no, Ali! I was just a little embarrassed, that's all. I turn red very easily." He smiled timidly, trying to look sincere.

She held her stare a little longer, and then flashed a smile, a big beautiful smile. "Okay, explanation accepted. Are you free tomorrow evening?" she asked enthusiastically.

John was stunned and at a loss for words. He had promised some of his golfing buddies that he would meet them for dinner and drinks at a local bar to begin planning their annual getaway golf trip to Doral. This planning session was a yearly ritual and something he never missed, but at this point he just couldn't say no to her. Trying to compose himself, he flashed a silly grin and replied. "Uh...sure, I'm open. What do you have in mind?"

"How about a movie? There's a movie I've been wanting to see and it's playing at Sumter Landing, and then later on we could go dancing at City Fire."

It was as if she was saying, *Now that I've got you where I want you, here's the plan.*

"Sounds good." John couldn't believe what he was saying—he hated dancing.

"Oh, wonderful! I live in a garage apartment at my aunt's house on Lake Harris. Her address is 1242 Lakeshore Drive."

"Great," John replied. "I'll just plug her address in my GPS and see you tomorrow night."

Ali quickly snatched a little note pad from her purse and scribbled down her aunt's address and handed it to John. "The movie starts at seven, so how about picking me up at six sharp? We can grab some fast food and head for the movie."

"Six it is, and I love fast food." John rarely went to fast food restaurants, feeling that it was beneath him.

Ali jumped out of the SUV, and hurried to her car at the side of the building. No squeeze or peck on the cheek this time. *She's on to me, I'd better be on my best behavior tomorrow night,* he thought.

John's head was spinning; he had just been slashed to pieces and turned into a sniveling little wimp by the nicest, sweetest, most beautiful girl he had ever met. He watched as Ali drove past and exited the parking lot. Waiting a few seconds, he pulled out on 466 and gunned it down the busy boulevard toward Sumter Landing for what he hoped would be a night of serious drinking at Cody's Original Roadhouse.

Chapter 3

"Hey Lex, isn't that your old squeeze getting out of that white Escalade out front?"

Lex raised up from under the hood of the car, his eyes quickly darted through the open garage door to the front of the building. It was her alright, it was Ali. Stunned and shaken, he mumbled. "Could be Dave, not sure."

"Could be my ass, that's her! I put a battery in her car today. I thought that Honda looked familiar. And it looks like she's found a rich one this time!" Laughter filled the garage area as other men joined in the friendly harassment of their co-worker.

Lex felt like he had been punched him in the gut. It hurt terribly to see Ali with another man— especially some rich guy who didn't care a wit about her. Too upset to respond to the other men, he stuck his head back under the hood and continued working. The men, noticing his reaction, stopped ribbing him and also went back to work. A contrite Dave walked over near Lex and attempted to console his friend. "Forget her buddy, no girl's worth fretting about, not even one as pretty as her."

Lex didn't reply. He yanked the bolt tight on the carburetor, and without warning, slammed the hood down and tossed the wrench in the nearby toolbox. He glanced at his watch, "It's quittin' time," he said.

"It's only 4:45, Lex, last I heard we quit at five," Dave joked.

"Close enough," Lex mumbled. He ducked around Dave and quickly washed up in the sink next to his station. Without acknowledging the apologetic looks from Dave and the other men, he hurried out to the back parking lot and climbed into his vintage '96 Pontiac Firebird. The loud mufflers groaned as he started the powerful car, backed up and cruised past the front of the building. Upset and feeling sick inside, he gunned it onto 466 and headed for home.

He slipped on his sunglasses, leaned over and knuckled open the glovebox. Reaching inside, he carefully lifted out one of the joints that he had made early that morning before work. He grabbed his red plastic lighter from the glovebox, flicked it on and lit up. Using several quick drags to heighten the burn, he then paused and took a long, deep drag, holding it in until the hot smoke burned into his lungs. A short time later, he turned south onto 441 to start the last leg of his drive home.

With his senses beginning to numb, Lex gazed aimlessly at the road ahead. Still shaken by his encounter with Ali and the guy in the Caddy, past memories of he and Ali's tumultuous ten-year relationship flooded through his mind. The booze, the pot, the cross words, and all the broken promises came rushing back. He wished he could do it all over again, but that wasn't possible. His own poor decision making had caused him to lose the only girl he had ever truly loved.

After his breakup with Ali, his life had spiraled out of control. Depressed and badly shaken by the split, he had sought comfort in a life of alcohol and drugs. Eventually, his reckless and devil-may-care attitude led to two arrests for possession of marijuana. The coup de grace for this irresponsible behavior came a few months after their breakup when he moved from a drug user to a drug pusher. Short of cash, he was looking for a way to support his ever increasing affinity for pot and alcohol. Not a meth user himself, he knew that there was a high demand for it in the economically challenged central Florida area. The folks in this area couldn't afford cocaine or heroin, so they turned to the cheap and affordable methamphetamine, or crank, to ease their pain. After borrowing a few hundred bucks from his mom, Lex convinced a couple of friends to join him, and it wasn't long before he had a meth lab up and running in the garage of his rented condo.

For a while, the crank business was very good for Lex. It was not uncommon for him to bring in more than a thousand dollars a week when things were really rolling. But when a local task force was formed to fight the growing crank epidemic in the area, his business began to dry up. With the heat on and his cash flow down, Lex made the decision to cut his losses and get out of the crank business. Ironically, the very night he decided to get out of the business, was the night he got busted.

Alone in his condo, he had heard a quick knock on the door. He thought it was one of his customers stopping by to get resupplied, so he hurried over and answered the door. To his shock and surprise, he was greeted by two uniformed county sheriff's deputies. They immediately read him his rights, cuffed him and took him away. The next thing he knew, he was in the backseat of a squad car heading for the county jail. Two hours later, he was behind bars with a hundred-thousand dollar bail hanging over his head. Well known in the area, his arrests were a great embarrassment not only to him, but also to his friends and family.

Fortunately for Lex, with his meth business on the wane, he hadn't cooked any new stuff that day. After a thorough search of his garage that was adjacent to the condo, the cops were only able to find a trace of the drug in a couple of plastic pop bottles, a Class B felony. If it had been a big day of cooking, they would have found several ounces of meth in the garage, which would have been a Class A felony. A Class A felony could have gotten him twenty to thirty years in the slam, while a Class B was punishable by only five to ten.

The former local basketball sensation was now divorced, alone and in jail. Unable to make bond, he turned to his family for help, but unfortunately they weren't able to muster up the ten thousand necessary for bond either and Lex was forced to linger in jail for several months. To make matters worse, during his time in jail he was unable to make his condo payments. As a result, the contract holder called the contract due and took the condo back from Lex, leaving him homeless and in jail.

Because of Lex's financial woes, the county appointed him a public defender to represent him at trial. Only weeks away from a long overdue retirement, the aging attorney was forgetful and nearly deaf. The trial lasted just two days with the jury deliberating for only twenty minutes. Lex was found guilty and given five years in a federal penitentiary for methamphetamine trafficking. He was also ordered to pay the County Hazardous Waste Division for the yet-to-be determined costs of cleaning up the contamination in and around his former condo.

Surprisingly, his otherwise unimpressive attorney presented a strong argument at the sentencing hearing and the judge reduced the sentence from five to two years. The old attorney convinced the judge that even though Lex had a couple of misdemeanor pot convictions, the small amount of meth on the scene would be that of a purely recreational user and not a pusher. His argument convinced the judge and he reduced the sentence.

Lex was a model prisoner at the Florida Department of Corrections, volunteering for many work details and helping repair the prison's motor vehicles. With time off for good behavior, he was released after serving only twelve months of his two-year sentence. But all the news wasn't good, two days before his release, he received a bill from the County Health Department in the sum of fifty-two thousand dollars for cleaning up the contamination at his former condo.

Free, but now heavily in debt, he thought back to how grateful he had been when an old friend of the family offered him a job at Tire Hut as a mechanic. Known as a fine mechanic by everybody in the area, it was a good fit for him. Soon after starting the twelve-dollar an hour job, he was notified by the county court that his wages would be garnisheed to the tune of a hundred dollars a week until the contamination costs had been repaid fully to the county.

Unable to afford rent payments and not wanting

to live with his mother and endure her constant lectures, Lex began looking around for a place to live. He soon found an old beat-up mobile home at the end of a long lane in a heavily wooded area just south of Leesburg. The heating system consisted of a wood burning stove fueled by timber that he chopped from trees in the surrounding woods. His running water consisted of a two-inch well. An old hot water heater gave him barely enough hot water for a daily shower. Fortunately, his uncle owned the property, so he was able to live there rent free. After paying his garnishment each month, he barely had enough money left to live on.

But the worst part of his breakup was losing Ali. His feelings for her were so intense that he hurt inside. Still heartbroken by their breakup, it was a gut wrenching pain that wouldn't go away. Shamed by his jail time, and heavily in debt, he now had even less to offer a girl like Ali. His feelings of loss were constant and unrelenting. He often wondered if he would ever feel good again.

Arriving home, he flipped on his turn signal and headed down the grooved-out lanes toward his mobile home. Minutes later, the old Firebird chugged to a stop in front of the rusted trailer. His cell rang, he looked at the screen and answered, "Hey Rudy, what's up?"

"Where are ya?"

"Just got home."

"I called you three times today."

"You know I can't talk at work, I leave my cell in the car."

"What about lunch, you could have called me when you went out for lunch."

"I ate in the breakroom."

"The great Lex Higgins, former star athlete at Belleview High School, has got no time for his old friends." Rudy laughed sarcastically.

"Yeah, I'm a real star. Cut the bullshit, Rudy. What do you want?" Phone to his ear, Lex climbed out of the car and made his way toward the front door.

"How are things working out for you lately, Lex?"

"Okay, I'm fine."

Rudy grunted, "Great digs you're livin' in, nice trailer. I'd say you're doing real well."

Lex stopped on his way to the door, "I'm hot and tired, so cut the insults, alright!"

There was a pause on the other end, "Listen friend, we've got a big operation running on an abandoned farm just outside of Oxford. Sometimes on a Friday night we have two labs goin'. I'm pulling in over two grand a week."

Lex knew what Rudy wanted, he exhaled and fell against his broken storm door. He was conflicted, he hated being broke all the time. He couldn't afford to go to dinner or to take a girl on a date, or anything else for that matter, but he couldn't go back to selling meth—he just couldn't. "Like I say, Rudy, I'm doing fine."

Sensing the hesitation, Rudy pressed on. "You're the best, Lex, the stuff we're making now ain't worth a shit. People are complaining, we need better stuff. You could make some extra cash, get a new car, and get out of that dump you're living in. How about it?"

"No fuckin' way, Rudy! I've been to jail once, that's enough for me! I have to go, bye."

He ended the call and looked out over the tall grass swaying gently in the large field next to his place. The scene was so peaceful, yet inside he felt such turmoil. "Damn him!" he groused. He pulled the rickety storm door open and stepped inside—a thick musty smell filled his nostrils. "What a dump," he mumbled.

He tossed his car keys on the kitchen table knocking over a couple of empty beer cans. There was a half-smoked joint lying in a dirty ashtray on the table. He lifted it up, flicked his lighter on and lit up. He took a huge drag, fell down in his worn out recliner and just stared at the ceiling fan rotating above. "I'll always love you, babe, I always will!" he moaned, dragging hard on his joint. "That rich bastard's not going to steal my girl from me," he growled. He angrily snatched his morning coffee cup from the small table next to his chair, leaned up and threw it violently against the far wall. The cup exploded into a hundred pieces, several dark streams of coffee wound their way down the dirty white paneling.

Chapter 4

"Got another Bud back there, Fritz?"

"You're hitting it kind of hard tonight, John. Tough week at the bank?"

"Yes, but that's not what's bugging me."

"Want to talk about it?" Fritz set a cold draft on the bar in front of Cullen."

John lifted the mug and took a sip and sat it gently on the bar. "Know a girl named Ali Brenneman?"

Fritz stopped wiping the counter and stared at John. "Who doesn't?"

John's brow lifted, "Oh yeah?"

"Yeah, she's great looking and nice to boot. Are you seeing her? She's kind of young for you."

"Not really. I met her last week and we went to Ocala shopping today, and we're going to a movie tomorrow night."

Fritz chuckled, "I never thought I would see you take a girl to the movie, she must have really tripped your trigger!"

"No way! It's just that she likes movies, that's all."

"I hear ya, but just be careful, my friend. She's broken a lot of hearts around here."

"Really?"

"Yeah, especially one."

John's eyes narrowed.

"Her ex-husband, a local guy named Lex Higgins. We all went to high school together. She was the star on the girls' basketball team and he was the star on the boys' basketball team. They were the perfect couple."

"What happened?"

"This will take a while, ya' got a minute?"

"I've got all night."

Fritz gave the bar a few more slow swipes and leaned against the cooler. "It was one of those high school love affairs, if you know what I mean."

John nodded.

"They started dating in the ninth grade and they both seemed to have bright futures ahead of them. They were smart, good-looking and popular. I'm sure both of their parents had high hopes for them, but sadly, that's not how it worked out."

"Tell me about it." John took a sip of his beer and looked intently at Fritz.

Fritz gave John an "if you insist look" and went on.

"It started with Ali's father. He was a great guy. Everybody liked Dutch Brenneman. Have you ever met anyone that just lights up a room when they walk in?"

"Sure."

"Well, that was Old Dutch. He never knew a stranger. Then one day at work he started having chest pains. The pains got so bad they rushed him to the hospital. There was no emergency EMS around here in those days and the hospital was twenty miles away, so as you might guess, Dutch never made it to the emergency room. He had a massive heart attack on the way and died instantly. He was just in his mid-fifties. It was sad, it was a real loss. He was the plant manager at a successful furniture company in Leesburg and made good money."

"He sounds like quite a guy."

"He was, and Ali was devastated by his death."

"I'm sure."

"But there's more."

John's chin raised begging more information.

"Like I said, Dutch made good money. He drove a big Mercedes and he and his wife had a big house over near Belleview, but I'm afraid Dutch had a problem—a big problem. We all found out later that he was frequenting the dog tracks in Tampa and filling out every tip sheet he could get his hands on. After the dust settled and all the bills were paid, Old Dutch had left his wife pretty much flat broke. He had a small life insurance policy at the plant, but she had to use that to pay for his funeral. She found out later that the house in Belleview was pretty much mortgaged to the hilt. She really loved that house, but she couldn't afford to pay all the loans against it, so she had to sell her beloved house and move into a much smaller place in Fruitland Park. Ali's dreams of going to college and playing basketball were over. She was offered a few small scholarships from private schools, but they weren't nearly enough to cover the total cost of college. After a brief stint at a beauty school, she dropped out and started working odd jobs around town. That's what she has been doing ever since."

"That's a bummer. What about her boyfriend? What's his story?"

"It's not much better. He was driving in for a layup in the final game of the sectional in his senior year and injured his leg. It turned out to be a badly torn Achilles tendon. He had surgery and after several months of rehab, things were starting to look up. But then he injured it again playing in a summer league and that was it, his leg was never the same after that. He had a few more surgeries, but it didn't help. It was a shame; he had several major colleges interested in him before the injury. His folks didn't have much money, so without a basketball scholarship, college was out of the question for him. He and Ali continued dating and they finally got married when they were around twenty. Neither one of them had a good job, and they really struggled. Lex was a pretty big drinker, even back then. Rumor has it that he was running around on Ali and got involved with a lady bartender in The Villages, although I can't prove that."

John shook his head, "What happened next?"

"After a tumultuous ten years, the marriage finally broke up. Ali tried to make things work, but Lex couldn't get off the booze and drugs, so she finally decided to cut her losses and go her own way. He was devastated by the divorce and has never gotten over it to this day."

"When was the divorce?"

"About three years ago."

"Sad story. "

"Yeah, Lex and I were good friends in high school and we stayed pretty close after that. He used to come in here quite a bit, but after the break up with Ali, he only came in occasionally. Sadly, he got in with the wrong crowd and got involved with meth."

"Wow, meth, not good." John paused as if deep in thought and then smiled at the talkative bartender. "Thanks for all the info, buddy."

"Anytime, and if you don't mind, could I offer you a little advice?"

John's brow lifted.

"If I were you, I would steer clear of Lex. He's extremely jealous of Ali and he's got a mean streak in him."

John grimaced. "Has he ever gone after anybody?"

"Yeah, he got into it with a guy in here one night. Ali came in with this fella for a drink and as you might know, it was one of the rare nights when Lex had stopped in for a drink." Fritz nodded to his left. "He was down there at the end of the bar and was feeling no pain. Unfortunately, he saw Ali and her date right away. His eyes locked on them like magnets. He just sat there glaring at them. I think seeing her with another man was more than the poor bastard could bear. All of a sudden, he walked over to Ali and asked her to step outside so he could talk to her. She said no, but Lex persisted. Finally her date told Lex to back off. Words were exchanged and before I knew it, they were at each other's' throats. I broke it up right away, but I'll never forget the look on Lex's face. It was pure evil."

John looked concerned. "What's he doing now?"

"He's a mechanic down at Tire Hut."

John chuckled nervously, "You don't say? We took Ali's car there today to have a new battery installed."

"Good chance he saw you."

John shook his head. "Hope not. Tell me, Fritz, do you think this guy would come after me?"

"Not sure, she's dated a couple of local guys since that night without any problems, but a rich banker in a new Escalade might be a different story." Fritz tapped John's forearm. "Just be careful."

"Warning accepted," John smiled meekly. Fritz's warning added another layer of uncertainty to John's already uncomfortable relationship with Ali. He would take note, but he wasn't sure if he would be able to pull back from her or not, even if it meant a possible problem with a jealous ex-husband.

Suddenly, there were voices in the background. Fritz looked past John toward the front door. "The usual fellas?"

"Yeah, and give one to our friend here, he looks lonesome."

John turned at the sound of the familiar voices, "Dave! Ed! What a surprise, how are you guys?"

"Great John, we just played eighteen at Palmer. Thought we'd stop and have a few," Dave replied. "You said you had a date tonight. Where's the girl? In the ladies room?"

"Oh...uh no, we went to Ocala shopping today and then she had a commitment with her mother tonight."

His friends hopped on the stools on either side of John. "Woo! Sounds like you got shot down, pal!" Ed exclaimed.

John squirmed, "Not exactly, I just misunderstood her plans for the day."

"Was it that girl you left Cody's with last Saturday night?" Ed offered.

"Yeah, same one."

"She's a real looker."

John nodded.

"She dumped you for her mother—you must have impressed the hell out of her," Dave needled his old friend.

John's face flushed with annoyance, "She had a good time smart ass. I'm going out with her tomorrow night."

"Tomorrow night? We were going to have dinner at the country club and go over our trip to Doral. Remember?"

"I know, I'm sorry about that. This just came up at the last minute."

Ed reached over and punched Dave in the shoulder. "I guess we know where we stand."

John shook his head.

"Must be love," Dave cried.

"No way, Davey! A few roles in the hay and I'm on my way."

"I dunno, that girl looked special to me and she's so young. I don't think I could handle something like that."

John smiled at his friend. "She's just another wannabee," John's voice trailed off, denying his bravado.

"Whoa! Another wannabee!" Ed howled.

"Some of us got it and some of us don't!" John retorted.

"Some got it and some don't, my foot!" Dave exclaimed sarcastically. "Listen Romeo, they're all after your money and you know it. They all want to marry you and live in that big house of yours. They dream of sitting on your big deck with a glass of wine in their hand and watching the sunset over that beautiful golf course."

John laughed and gave the middle finger to his golfing buddy. "And I suppose those hangers-on you've been dating are enamored by your wonderful personality and not that new Mercedes!"

"Hangers-on, is it?"

"Yes, I would say that's pretty accurate," John said. All three men roared while high-fiving one another.

"I guess we're just a miserable bunch of dirty old men," Dave uttered through the laughter.

"Yea, but ain't it fun," John replied.

"Ladies beware!" Dave bellowed. The men touched glasses, sucked down their drafts and slammed them on the bar. Fritz hurried over and replaced them with three foamy refills. The three good friends laughed and chided one another and continued drinking until the wee hours of the morning.

Chapter 5

The wobbly screen door creaked open. "Here kitty, kitty." A plump calico cat meowed loudly just before darting through the partially open front door. Ali yawned mightily, scratched the side of her head, and looked out the door at the beautiful sunrise glistening on the nearby lake. With an approving smile on her face, she pulled the door shut, walked over to her under-sized kitchen with Formica countertops and reached inside the faded cabinet just above the kitchen sink. Needing a cup of coffee, she reached in the cabinet and pulled out a cup with a 7-11 logo printed on the side. She lifted the warm pot from the still brewing coffee machine next to the sink and splashed her cup full. She sauntered into the tiny living room, coffee in hand, and plopped down in an old, over-sized chair that she borrowed from her mother a few years ago. Lifting the TV remote from a metal TV tray that doubled as her end table, she clicked on the television. A snowy picture with red lines running across it slowly came into view. She clicked on the local news channel and took a sip of coffee. Not unexpectedly, her iPhone sitting on the TV tray next to her began to ring. The sound of "Start Me Up" by the Stones soon filled the room. She lifted the phone and punched it on.

"Good morning, Mom. Yes, the doors are locked, Mom." Ali looked over as a morning breeze pushed her rickety screen door open ever so slightly.

"Don't worry, I won't be late for work, Mom. I haven't been late for work in five years, so you really don't need to call me every morning to remind me." Ali shook her head. "I know you worry about me living alone, but really, I'm doing just fine.

She listened patiently to the "since your father died you're my responsibility" diatribe she had heard almost every morning since her father's death, even when she was married to Lex. That's why she had moved into the garage apartment at her Aunt Ella's place on Lake Harris after the divorce—to get away from mom. But, even though her mom was a pain in the backside, she was still the only person who cared enough about her to call and check on her every day and she loved her for that.

"You have to be careful, there's all kinds of people out there nowadays, you know."

"I know, Mom. Bye, Mom, gotta go. Love you."

After hanging up Ali suddenly felt all alone. She was close to her Aunt Ella, but her aunt worked long hours and what little free time she had was taken up by her own children and grandchildren. The only time Ali saw her aunt was when she came out to the garage on Sunday morning to go to church. Ali ran a register at CVS in The Villages and her work day was from eight to four. Her aunt worked second shift at a local hospital from three to eleven. An occasional "hi, how are you," was about the only communication the two of them shared.

Embarrassed by her meager living quarters, Ali didn't invite many guests to her little apartment. She even went so far as to have her dates pick her up at her mom's home in Fruitland Park, about ten miles north of Lake Harris. The problem with that was her overprotective mom was always butting in and asking her dates awkward questions. Hating these embarrassing intrusions from mom, she reluctantly decided to have her dates pick her up at her own apartment—embarrassing or not.

An honor student and an outstanding athlete in high school, Ali had shown great promise as a youngster. But her father's tragic death when she was only seventeen left her mother broke and without the resources to send her to college. Any thoughts of a bright future were dashed by her father's untimely passing.

Having only a high school education to her credit, Ali found it difficult to find a good paying job in the local area. As a result, she soon found herself working at CVS for nine dollars an hour—barely enough to put gas in the car, pay for groceries and take care of the utilities at her apartment. Attractive and well spoken, she felt her only chance to get ahead in life was to find a good husband. After several brief flings with some local blue-collar guys, she decided to try her luck with an older more established man. The resulting quest found her spending quite a bit of time in bars and night spots of a nearby retirement community called The Villages. Her favorite haunt was a popular local hangout named Cody's Original Roadhouse. That's where she had met John Cullen the week before.

Ali liked her possibilities with Cullen. He was somewhat arrogant and controlling, but that was typical for most wealthy men. Once she got to know him better, she was certain she would find him to be just like everyone else, suffering from the same doubts and insecurities. On the positive side, she liked what she saw with John. He was a handsome man and his nicely shaped mouth curved so easily into a smile. He also appeared to have the one quality she was looking for most in a man—generosity. In addition to eagerly paying for her car repair, he also mentioned several charities to which he donated, including World Vision and the Salvation Army.

To get ready for the big date tonight, she had stopped on the way home to buy a new pair of jeans. She had tried on several pairs, finally deciding on a pair that was a little snug around her bottom; a bottom that she knew John had spent a great bit of time ogling during their recent day at Ocala. While not overtly sexual, she enjoyed being a little flirtatious with the men she dated, but that's where she drew the line. Casual sex was not in the books for Ali Brenneman. There had to be love and commitment in a relationship before she would have sex with a man. And the proof was in the pudding; the only man she had ever been intimate with was her ex-husband, Lex Higgins. A man she had loved very deeply at one time.

This attitude had caused Ali her share of problems over the years. Feeling frustrated and rejected, most of her over-heated suitors would eventually give up on her and look for more submissive mates. But Ali remained undeterred by their rebuffs, she had seen too many of her sexually active girlfriends end up hurt and abandoned. Ali thought too highly of herself to let that happen.

The late night trip to John's house last weekend was out of character for Ali, and it caused her some uneasiness that John might think something had happened that night. In reality, he had passed out drunk while showing her his bedroom at three in the morning. Being a little mischievous by nature, she also found it slightly amusing for John to think their relationship may have been intimate, but she also knew that when push came to shove, she would definitely tell him the truth. She had worked way too hard to earn her good reputation to let one unfortunate evening mess things up.

Chapter 6

"Good morning, Mr. Morris. How is everything down at the bank?"

"Oh good, Ali, thanks for asking. How are you?"

"I'm just fine, keepin' busy, you know."

"I'll bet, fighting off all those men and looking after your mom like you do can't be easy."

Ali smiled.

"And how is Sally these days? I haven't seen her in quite a while," the friendly banker inquired.

"Fine, thanks. She gets a little lonely now and then, but she's doing okay." Ali rang up the mouthwash and toothpaste for Mr. Morris, slipped the items in a plastic bag and handed him the bag and his change.

"Please tell her hello the next time you see her."

"Sure will, and nice talking with you, Mr. Morris.

Have a nice day."

A line was starting to form at the register and Ali was anxious to get to the next customer. Mr. Morris glanced over his shoulder at those waiting, said a quick good-bye and left the counter.

Ali greeted the next customer. "Hi, Shirley, how are you today?" Ali quickly scanned her five items and dropped them in a bag.

"Good, thanks."

"Is this debit or credit?"

"Credit."

Shirley slid her card through the machine.

"Please punch credit and then sign on the screen." No matter how many times she came through the line, Shirley always forgot the procedure for signing her credit card. Ali patiently waited as she slowly scribbled her name.

"You have a good day, Shirley."

"You too, Ali." Shirley stuck her billfold in her purse and hurried off.

Ali suddenly felt weak, her stomach drew up into her throat. The next customer appeared from behind the somewhat expansive Shirley and stepped up to the counter. Ali collected herself and slowly stammered, "Well...uh hi, Lex. What are you doing here?"

"Hell, it's a drugstore, Ali. I thought it was open to the public." He shook his head disgustedly and dropped a case of Bud Light on the counter.

Ali nervously ran the scanner across the top of the beer cans. Since their divorce three years ago, this was the first time Lex had come to her workplace. They had an unspoken agreement to avoid coming face to face with one another if at all possible. She felt anxious and somewhat angry at the intrusion. She serviced her car at Tire Hut, but Lex worked in the shop, so the chance of a direct contact with one another was minimal. Plus, there were other drugstores in The Villages, but only one garage. She avoided eye contact with him, concentrating on the white tape as it climbed out of the cash register. She ripped it loose and handed it to him.

He grabbed her hand and held it firmly, "Could we talk sometime?"

Ali's hand was aching, but when she looked into his eyes, her mood softened. She shifted uneasily, not knowing how to respond. A sense of concern suddenly ran through her. She was overcome with a deep and gripping sadness as she gazed into his dark bloodshot eyes. His face looked thin and exhausted, nothing like the handsome young man she had loved for so many years. As exasperating as he could be, she would always have feelings for Lex Higgins. She couldn't help it. Her eyes clouded over, she spoke tenderly, "Are you okay, Lex?"

Her kind response startled him and he let go of her hand. His eyes turned shiny, he paused to collect himself. It was evident to Ali that he was still desperately in love with her. Never having to confront him face to face, she had convinced herself that he had gotten over her and was going on with his life. She felt an overwhelming sense of empathy for him as he spoke while fighting back the tears. "Oh, I just thought it...uh wouldn't hurt to kind of catch up on things, if you know what I mean." His voice began to weaken; it was obvious that he knew this could never happen. To Ali, it was heartbreaking. Tears rolled down her face. The girl in the camera shop looked over at Ali, and sensing her despair, hurried over to open another register. She called the customers behind Lex over to her register.

"Oh, Lex, I'm so sorry, but I really don't...."

His chin fell to his chest. Without lifting his eyes, he slid the case of beer from the counter and hurried away.

Ali held the receipt in her hand. "Lex, you forgot your...." She never finished the sentence. She watched as he walked quickly toward the door. His hair was long and scraggily, his wrinkled t-shirt that hung loosely on his boney back was soiled and full of holes, his worn out jeans were faded and baggy in the rear. Ali slipped a hanky from her smock and dabbed her eyes. She heard a car door slam and then the roar of mufflers followed by squealing tires. She stared aimlessly at the front glass as the angry growl of worn-out mufflers faded in the distance.

"You okay?" the girl at the next register asked.

Ali forced a smile, "Yes, I'm okay, Katie, thanks for opening up."

"You've covered my butt enough times, don't mention it."

Ali gently dropped Lex's receipt in the wastebasket beneath the counter and hurried back to the card section to continue restocking. She was overcome with grief; her heart was breaking. She had wanted very much to hold him and love him and tell him everything would be okay—like she used to do. But she knew that was impossible, too much had happened between them. Too many arguments, too many harsh words, too many drug related problems. Things could never work out between them, and she knew it, but she still hurt. The pain was so intense she could barely stand it. She could only imagine how he must feel. His life was falling apart and the only girl he had ever loved would have nothing to do with him. She wanted to scream, throw herself on the floor and pound it until her hands were bruised and bloody, but that wouldn't accomplish anything—she had a life to lead and a job to do. "God help him," she murmured as she carefully opened a package of American greeting cards and began shoving them on the shelf.

Chapter 7

Perspiration was pouring down John's face. His legs ached as he made his way up the last incline on the warm Florida morning. Arriving at the end of the driveway to his house, as always he stopped and slid the towel from his shoulders and dried his face. John ran four miles every morning before work. The last and most challenging leg of the journey was a two hundred yard dash up a modest incline that landed him about a hundred feet from the entrance to his estate. He slipped his hand in the pocket of his running tights and lifted out a small remote control and punched the button. The large iron gate that protected the long drive leading up to his mansion moved slowly open. Exhausted from his run, he paused to get his breath. It was his custom to give himself a chance to cool down by walking through the gate and up the winding cobblestone roadway to his house. It also gave him an opportunity to admire the large home that he and his ex-wife had built together a year before their divorce. He never grew tired of looking at his three-million dollar creation. Somehow it made him feel good inside, if only temporarily.

His mansion in the suburbs of Tampa was indeed impressive. Four huge white pillars surrounded the front of the ten-thousand square foot stucco home. The entryway included two large mahogany front doors with glass centers filled with decorative wrought iron. The impressive doors were tucked squarely in the center of a twenty by thirty foot glass entryway. Looking inside, the viewer's eyes were treated to a stunning marble bust of a young Augustus Caesar sitting on a mahogany stand in the center of a sunken living room covered by Calacatta marble imported from Italy. Past the bust and through the all-glass rear of the house, you could see an enormous fountain which was centered by a statue of a nude Adam standing in the Garden of Eden.

John reached the front door, walked through the living area and looked out the sliding door at the backyard. Adam's fountain was surrounded by long walkways that meandered through the two-acre estate. The walkways were bordered on both sides by over one-hundred species of different plants and flowers indigenous to central Florida. Bricked-in landscape areas and several smaller fountains were scattered throughout the yard. The fountains were strategically located to draw the guests' attention toward a large gazebo in the southwest corner of the yard which was surrounded by several stone-crafted benches and chairs. This section included John's favorite—a fire pit where he would sit with friends on the stone benches and enjoy beer, hot dogs, s'mores and other favorite campfire foods. It was his opportunity for him to prove to his friends how down to earth he was in the midst of such over-the-top opulence.

John felt a vibration. He lifted his cell phone from the leather holder clipped to his waist and answered, "Yes, Evans, what is it?"

"Sorry to trouble you at home so early, but I just got a call from Steve Wilbur."

"Why would Steve be calling this early?"

"It was about our merger meeting today at ten."

Irritated, John interrupted, "Oh no, he's not backing out, is he?"

"Well, not exactly. He wants a five year employment guarantee for his senior officers instead of the three we offered."

"What?"

"Yes, he says two of them have kids in college and won't graduate for four or five years and he would like for them to have secure employment until their kids graduate. He says it's non-negotiable."

"Non-negotiable! Why that shriveled-up old fart! Who does he think he is?"

"He's the president of the largest bank in Jacksonville with forty-seven branches and we're trying to get a foothold in that area."

John strolled over and plopped down on a sofa in the center section next to Caesar. He slid the towel from around his neck and dabbed the perspiration from his forehead. "Our project analysis showed his top people to be incompetent, except for that one girl, uh..."

"Julie Winston."

"Yes, yes, Julie Winston. She was sharp as a tack. She kept the whole place running, if you ask me."

"She was impressive, that's for sure. So what do you want me to do?"

"I don't like other people setting the agenda, Evans."

"I know, Mr. Cullen."

John glanced up at his hero Augustus. "Tell him it's no deal, it's three years—take it or leave it."

"But, sir, it's the largest...."

"You heard me, no deal. Our offer is two dollars a share more than anyone else has offered up to this point. With his holdings, he stands to become a very rich man along with most of his board. I really don't think his board would approve of him trying to nix this deal at the last moment. They have too much to lose.

"Yes, but five year guarantees are not unusual. In fact, most banks go five years and with the economy the way it is, it will be extremely difficult for his officers to find positions anywhere near to what they have now. That area has been hard hit by the recession."

"You heard me."

"I heard you, sir, but he sounded so determined. I think he may be able to convince his board to side with him."

"I don't think so. He needs the money too badly."

"He appears to be doing alright to me."

"But there's something you don't know, Evans."

"Oh?"

"Yes. You see a realtor friend of mine told me that Steve has put an offer in on a large home in Sarasota. The realtor told me that he has wanted this place for as long as he can remember and it just came on the market a few weeks ago. The closing is in two weeks and the selling price was over two million. Steve is doing okay, but I'm sure he doesn't have that kind of money lying around."

The phone fell quiet on the other end.

"Are you there, Evans?"

A distant sounding voice replied, "Yes, yes, I'm here."

"You have to toughen up, Evans, business is business."

"Those are nice folks up there in Jacksonville. I've

met with them several times and they have been very square with us. I simply don't think his request should be a deal breaker. We've certainly done it before. We gave your good friend at City National Bank a seven year contract."

John's face flushed red with anger. He liked Josh Evans, he was one of his best and most trusted employees, but he had gone too far in John's eyes with his last comment. "We gave Tower seven years because they had an exceptional staff."

"Exceptional? Mr. Cullen, you ended up buying all of them out with an early retirement deal just to get rid of them. That was a weak staff."

Seething, John wondered what Augustus would have done if a subordinate had challenged him like Evans had just done.

He sat up on the edge of the sofa and replied stiffly, "Listen, Evans, you've made your point. Anymore discussion about this and you'll be looking for a job."

No pushover, he knew that Evans would be somewhat taken aback by the threat, but he paid him well and when push came to shove, he was certain that he would back down.

Then came an almost inaudible reply, "You're the boss."

"Good, I will see you in about an hour. Good-bye."

"Good-bye."

John hurried from the living room toward his

bedroom to shower and get ready for work. He had barely gotten in front of the bedroom door when his phone began to ring again. He looked at the number. It was one he didn't recognize. He started to turn his phone off when he realized that the area code on the number was the same area code as his Village home. He wondered if the call was from Ali. Not wanting to take a chance on missing a call from her, he punched the phone on.

"Hello?"

"Good morning, John. I'm sorry for calling you so early, but you did tell me that you were an early riser."

John paused and sat down on the corner of his bed, "Oh, no problem, I just returned from my morning run. I've been up for over an hour."

"Oh good! It's nothing important really. You left your sunglasses on the little table by the front door to my apartment Saturday night. They look very expensive and you said you wouldn't be up for a couple of weeks. I called to see if you want me to mail them to you. You could have them by tomorrow."

The sound of Ali's voice was very soothing and seductive. John found himself wanting to talk to her longer. "Oh no, that's no problem. I didn't even realize I had left them there. I always carry an extra pair in my car."

"Okay, maybe you can pick them up the next time you are in town. Well, I'd better go or I'm going to be late for work."

"It was nice hearing your voice," he said softly.

"Oh, you're so sweet. I hope you enjoy your golf outing next weekend."

Every year John sponsored a weekend outing for the young executives at the bank. They drank beer, played golf and then everyone went home in an effort to sober up before work on Monday. It was his gig, so he felt he had to be there. "I'd rather be coming to The Villages," he replied.

"I'd rather you would be also," Ali said gently.

"This golf thing, it's my party, you know, so I feel I need to be there."

"I understand, and I will still be here in two weeks, so don't lose my phone number."

"Oh, don't worry, you're the first one on my speed dial." John lied. Until this call he didn't even have her cell number.

"Aww, you're so sweet. Have fun at your outing. Bye, John."

Now standing by his bed, John's legs felt weak. The unexpected "sweet" comment had him back on his heels. He wanted more than anything to see her this weekend. He struggled for his words, "Uh...bye."

John stood still and took a deep breath. He hadn't even kissed this girl and yet she had him literally in a fog.

After the break-up with his wife, he had promised himself that he would not get serious with anyone, ever again. The expensive divorce had made him angry at his wife and at odds with women in general. For him, women had become simply a diversion, a means for selfish pleasure. And so far, his plan had been working out just fine. He couldn't count the number of young unsuspecting women he had ravaged in the past four years since his divorce. But now, much to his chagrin, he could feel the tables turning. A working class girl in a beat-up Honda Civic had him dancing like a helpless puppet at the end of a string. A control freak by nature and a womanizer extraordinaire, he was having a difficult time comprehending what was happening to him. A part of him was frightened by Ali, but a part of him was completely enamored by her. As he peeled off his running tights and stepped into the shower to get ready for work, he was trying desperately to think of some way to get out of that golf outing next weekend. It wouldn't be easy, but he had to find a way. He had to see that pretty face and those sexy legs again—and soon.

Chapter 8

"You just don't look good, dear, that's all I'm saying. You're too thin."

"Don't worry, Mom, I'm okay, I've been working a lot of hours and I haven't been getting enough sleep."

"It's Ali, isn't it? You're thinking about Ali again, aren't you?"

"Mom, it's not Ali," he said almost inaudibly.

Her eyes moist, Lex's mom shook her head. "It's no use, son, you have to forget her. She always thought she was better than you anyway. You could never give her what she wanted. She's a Prima Donna."

"Don't say that, Mom! She's a good person!"

Lex was irritated by his mom's criticism of Ali. After one last tug on the wrench, he pulled himself out from under the kitchen sink, quickly stood and turned on the water. He dropped down on one knee and surveyed the elbow joint looking for any sign of a leak. Reaching his hand under the sink, he felt to see if there was any moisture around the connection in the drainage pipe. Feeling none, he stood and turned off the water. "There ya go, Mom, you're all set."

"Thanks, honey."

"I better get going."

"No time for coffee?"

"Not today."

"I'm sorry, dear, I know you still love Ali. Please forgive me. I should have kept my mouth shut. I don't know what I'd do without you to come over and fix things for me. With your dad gone, you're all I've got."

"I know, Mom, and don't worry, I'm not going anywhere."

"Thank you, honey, thank you." She rushed over and gave Lex a long fervent hug.

Lex pulled away and gave his mom a quick peck on the forehead. "I gotta go, Mom, I'll be late for work. See you Wednesday for tacos and don't forget the refried beans!"

She smiled and nodded.

"And Mom...."

She gazed intensely at her son, "Yes?"

"Don't say anything bad about Ali again, okay?"

"I won't, deary, I promise. She's a wonderful girl."

"Bye, Mom."

"Good-bye, son."

Lex quickly gathered up his tool belt and hurried out to his car. He jumped in on the driver's side and tossed his tool belt on the other seat. Gravel flew as he peeled away from his mother's house and headed for work. Lex didn't want his mom living in Brown's Trailer Court; the place had a dubious reputation. On disability due to a bad case of smoking induced emphysema, it was all she could afford. Lex worried about his mom—he worried about her living conditions and he worried about her health. He gave her a little money now and then, but it wasn't much. He wished he could do more, but he couldn't, and that bothered him a lot.

His mother had always dreamed of Lex becoming a professional person—maybe a doctor or an attorney. And Lex had shown great promise in high school. Majoring in college prep, he had received high marks in math and science and scored a respectable 1150 on his SAT, but a devastating injury to his leg during a basketball game during his senior year would change his life dramatically. His father, who died in an auto accident, had never been able to hold steady employment and didn't have any life insurance when he died. After his death, his mom quit her part-time job at the Sheriff's Department and went to work at a local boat company. But even with a full-time job, she could barely pay the bills. It didn't take long for Lex to realize that he would never be able to go to college.

Lex's phone rang. He picked it up and glanced at the screen. "What do you want? I'm late for work."

"I know, I saw your car over at your mom's place."

"I was hoping that you hadn't noticed."

There was a pause on the other end, "Do you always have to be such a smart-ass, Lex?"

Lex sighed, "Sorry, Rudy, it just seems like every time you call I get a bad feeling inside."

"Gee, thanks a lot."

"Don't mention it."

"You may not realize it, Lex, but I'm the only person in this world who gives a shit about you."

That one hurt. With all of his problems with the law, most of his old buddies had quit calling him. The girls he had dated after his breakup with Ali were still around, but they had all moved on to greener pastures. Rudy truly was the only one he ever heard from, but it was for all the wrong reasons. Lex spoke in almost a whisper. "You're full of shit, Rudy, What do you want?"

Rudy coughed up a sarcastic chuckle. "Your mom needs help, Lex, her place is going to hell in a handbasket. Her mobe's falling apart and she told me the other day that when it rains, the roof leaks in the living room and bedroom. I cleaned her gas heater last weekend, it hadn't been cleaned in years. She also said that her toilet isn't flushing right and her pipes are leaking."

Lex flared with anger, embarrassed that a low-life

like Rudy was helping his mom. "You think I don't know that, Rudy? I've been over there five times to patch that roof! It's not perfect, but it's all she can afford right now."

"Maybe not."

"Don't go there, Rudy, it's no deal. I'll take care of my mom all right and I don't need your fucking drug money to do it."

"Listen, I used to work at Tire Hut. I know what you're making, so don't bullshit me."

"I gotta go." Lex clicked his phone off without waiting for Rudy's reply. His mind was racing. Rudy was right, his salary was barely enough to take care of his own meager living arrangements, let alone provide any financial assistance to his mom. And unfortunately, in his current condition, he was not in any position to find a better job. Ali's new boyfriend had him thrown off balance. He hadn't been eating or sleeping well lately and he had lost twenty pounds. He was really down and it was beginning to show at work. Always the perfectionist, he was starting to screw up and make mistakes.

If he took Rudy's advice and went back to cooking meth again, he could earn upwards of two-thousand dollars a week. That kind of cash flow would give him enough money to get his mom a better place and rent himself a condo on the lake. He could buy some new clothes and clean up and save enough to be able to fulfill his dream of opening his own Jiffy Lube—his first step toward getting Ali back.

The problem was, if he started cooking again he could end up back in jail. A convicted felon, if he got caught, they would throw the book at him. He would go back to the big house for a minimum of twenty years, maybe more. His insides were ripping apart as he accelerated down Highway 301 for the eight mile trip to work. It was already ten after eight. At this rate he would be twenty minutes late for work— something he could ill afford.

Lex tapped the steering wheel nervously and stared ahead at the approaching light. It turned red. The light would hold him up for a couple of minutes, so he slipped his cell phone from his pocket and called Rudy.

"Well hello, that was quick. Thought I might never hear from you again, at least I was hoping."

"Cut the crap, Rudy, I've got a few questions for you."

"Fire away. I'm just sitting here at home adding up my daily deposit for the bank. Let's see, the total today is three-hundred-sixty dollars."

The light changed, Lex accelerated through the intersection. "That's just one day?"

"Well, it's actually two, but I've had single days this big."

"The price of crank must have gone up."

"Not much, there's just a lot more users. People are sucking on plastic bottles like nobody's business.

I think they're more depressed because of the economy," he chuckled coarsely.

Lex's heart was racing. He knew what he was doing was wrong, but he was tired of being broke and unhappy, and he wanted desperately to get Ali back.

"Where did you say you were cooking now—some barn over by Oxford?"

"Yeah, it's on an old abandoned farm and its way back in a wooded area. The owner of the farm used to be my neighbor. He moved back to Chicago about five years ago and hasn't been back since. He calls me about once a year and asks me to drive by the farm and check things out, so I'm more or less the caretaker for the place. And better yet, you can't smell the meth from the road, even on a windy day. There's only one road leading to the barn and one road out and it's a half mile long. And get this, we installed an early warning system next to the road. Every time a vehicle starts down the lane, a camera-sensor beeps and we can look at a monitor in the barn and see who's coming—a little extra security."

"Pretty ingenious."

"Yeah, if the police would ever try a raid, we would just hop in our trucks and peel across a little backroad to 450N and we're out of there. By the time the fuzz would get to the barn and figure out what is going on, we would be long gone. We'd be history, man, history."

Lex had two more lights to negotiate before he got

to work, so he still had a few moments. "Hmm... sounds pretty secure."

"It is, buddy, it is. There's only four of us cooking now and we've never told anybody where we have the lab. We sell the stuff every day at various places and then we finish the week off at a boat company parking lot on Friday afternoon. That's our biggest day."

"Payday?"

"You got it. We get the poor bastards' money before they have a chance to use it for something else."

"Like paying the rent?"

"Maybe, that's their problem, not mine," Rudy grunted.

"You're a sweetheart."

"I suppose you didn't do shit like that, right? You only sold to folks who had a lot of money. You're no better than the rest of us, Lex."

Lex clammed up, he didn't have a reply. Everybody knew meth was the drug of choice for the downtrodden. Rudy was right, he was no better than anybody else who had ever trafficked crank.

"I'm losing my patience with you, Lex. Like I told you before, you're the best and my customers want your stuff again. They're not happy, but I'm tired of your crap and I want to know if you're in or out. If not, quit bothering me and I'll quit bothering you."

Lex pushed down the turn signal, cut across the

southbound lane and darted into the lot at Tire Hut. Rudy had called him out and he had very little time to digest everything. He didn't like being pressured, but Rudy sounded serious. "Well...uh."

"Spit it out, man, are you cooking or not?"

Lex looked inside the shop at the guys getting ready for another day of fixing flats, changing oil, and repairing old beat-up cars that were ready for the junk heap and then trying to explain to the owner why something wasn't fixed right. All of the men had dour looks on their faces. It was a hot, dirty and stressful job that paid barely above minimum wage and offered very little hope for promotion. A frown spread across Lex's face. "Okay, Rudy, I'm in on one condition."

"Okay, what's the condition?" Rudy sounded eager.

"I want a fourth of everything I cook."

"A fourth, my ass! Nobody gets a quarter of the take!"

"I'm taking an awful risk here, Rudy."

Rudy groaned and then got quiet for a moment. "You're full of shit, Lex, but you're the best, so I'll think about it."

"When will you call?"

"I'll let you know tonight, good-bye." Rudy abruptly hung up, obviously not happy about Lex's condition. But Lex needed to make lots of money. If the money wasn't there, he wouldn't take the chance.

Turning the ignition key off, the big engine groaned to a stop. He hurried inside to face another long day at work.

Chapter 9

Ned Carpenter stepped out of the back of his house and paused just outside the sliding glass doors. The cool morning breeze gave off a chill that smelled of dampness. It was barely seven o'clock on Friday morning and the morning sun was just starting to spread its golden rays over the horizon at Lake Miona. Ned flinched as two Sandhill Cranes flew over honking, as if angered by Ned's intrusion into their early morning space. From a patch of lily pads near a stand of Queen Palms, croaking bull frogs treated him to a morning serenade. With wings flapping backward, several Mallard ducks glided to a stop on the nearby lake. "It's paradise," he sighed.

Ned felt very blessed to live in The Villages in such a wonderful neighborhood. It was a dream come true for him and his wife, Ellie. When his father died several years ago at the ripe old age of eighty-nine, he left Ned, who was then near retirement age himself, a surprisingly big inheritance. It was more than enough to allow Ned and his wife to fulfill their dream of owning their own home in The Villages.

Prior to retirement, Ned had spent the bulk of his forty year career with the local Sheriff's Department in Leesburg. He knew most of the folks in Leesburg on a first name basis and over the years had developed a reputation as a likeable and fair law enforcement official. He ran for sheriff the year before his father's death and was barely defeated in the close race. Exhausted by the long and difficult campaign, after much thought and discussion with friends and family, Ned decided to hang it up and retire from law enforcement.

Although not a wealthy man by any standard, his retirement pension provided Ned with sufficient funds to maintain his debt-free home in Bridgeport and still have enough money left to enjoy the many sights and sounds of his beloved Villages.

Ned loved the surroundings at his new home, especially the lake. A lifelong fisherman, he could now indulge in his favorite activity any time he wanted. With that in mind, he hurried off the deck, grabbed his fishing pole off the corner of the steps and walked briskly toward the lake. Arriving at the water, he unhooked the artificial bait from the pole and made his first cast. Reeling it in, he watched as the gleaming bait wiggled its way across the still water.

Preparing to cast again, his attention was drawn to a familiar sound coming from the front of the house near the road. He turned to look between the houses and caught a glimpse of a bright red Firebird cruising past his house. Ned knew that car; it belonged to a local guy named Lex Higgins. He recognized the bold pinstripes, tinted windows, and groaning mufflers. Ned's eyes narrowed. It was the second time this week he had seen Lex's car driving slowly around Bridgeport. Something didn't smell right to this old hound dog of a cop. Fishing pole in hand, he scurried up the slight incline to get a better look. Pausing briefly, to place his pole next to the stairs, he quickly continued toward the front of the house. Stopping at the corner of his front yard, he used a giant bougainvillea for cover. He gently pushed the red flowers apart and watched as the car roll slowly past.

Ned couldn't think of any good reason why Lex Higgins, a young man of little means, would be driving around Bridgeport this early in the morning. He stood still and watched as Lex suddenly came to an abrupt stop in front of a neighbor's large elaborate home. The house belonged to a Tampa banker named John Cullen. Ned had seen Lex pause near his house earlier in the week. He knew from years in law enforcement that this kind of behavior was out of the ordinary. Something wasn't right between Lex

Higgins and John Cullen.

Ned knew the Higgins' family. He had done a little fishing with Lex's father before he died, and Lex's mother, Carolyn, had worked for him in the Lake County Sheriff's department as a temp when Lex was in high school. During her stint in his office, Lex's mother would talk incessantly about her son. Being the star of the local high school basketball team and a very popular kid, Lex had shown a lot of promise. Unfortunately, her son injured his leg late in his senior year. After several surgeries and a lengthy rehab, his leg was never the same. Still hoping to attend college, the family was dealt a devastating blow when his father died unexpectedly a few weeks after Lex graduated. After his father's death, his dreams of going to college became pretty much a distant memory.

Later that summer, Lex attempted to move on with his life by marrying his high school sweetheart, Ali Brenneman. Sadly, after a tumultuous ten year relationship, their marriage ended in divorce. One of the prettiest girls in the entire area, Lex was never the same after their break-up. Devastated by the divorce and down on his luck, he had turned to drugs to ease the pain. It wasn't long before his name began showing up all too often on the department's daily arrest reports. It soon became pretty much common knowledge around the area that Lex Higgins, once a young man with so much promise, had become a troubled and possibly angry young man.

A reasonable man, Ned had more or less given Lex the benefit of the doubt the first time he drove through Bridgeport, dismissing it as an attempt by Lex to locate a house for a pick up by his auto garage later in the day. But the second trip convinced Ned that these visits by Lex had nothing to do with repairing John Cullen's car. A recent comment by one of the guys at the coffee shop in Leesburg only added to Ned's suspicions. The man's wife worked with Ali's mom, Sally. She confided to his wife that Ali had been seeing some rich dude in The Villages and that Lex was having a hard time with it. Ned surmised that this wealthy man must be Cullen. Ned could see a scenario developing in which Lex was so jealous and troubled by Ali's hook-up with Cullen that he felt compelled to do something about it. His gut told him that he needed to stay on top of this situation before somebody got hurt.

Several newspapers were scattered around the drive at the Cullen house, a sign that John hadn't been around for a while. A frequent visitor to his Village home, Ned knew that it would only be a matter of time before Cullen returned. He carefully released the limb of the bougainvillea and headed for the back of the house. On his way, he slid his cell phone out of his front pocket and punched in the number of the local sheriff's department.

Chapter 10

Ned was not looking forward to calling the current sheriff to discuss the Lex Higgins' situation. He held the cell phone to his ear and leaned back against the soft cushion. The grating ring of the old phone in his former work place pierced his ears.

Ned's relationship with the current Sheriff of Lake County was not as friendly as he would like. Ned and his retired boss, Sheriff Owen, had both grown up in the Leesburg area and were well-liked and respected by the natives of Leesburg. The current sheriff, Dave Cline, was a transplant from nearby Orange County, and did not enjoy the same level of acceptance as his predecessors. His lack of acceptance by the locals bothered the sheriff. As a result, he rarely asked for an opinion or guidance on local law enforcement issues from Ned or Sheriff Owen.

"Good morning, Sheriff's Department."

"Oh hi, Susie, Ned Carpenter here."

"Why Ned, how are you? How's my favorite deputy doing these days with retirement and all?'

"Great, Susie, I golf 'bout every day."

"How are you hittin' 'em?"

"Often."

She chuckled. "What can I do for you today, Ned?"

"Boss in?" Ned's free hand tapped nervously on the metal arm of the chair. Something inside him was almost hoping that Susie would say no.

"Yes, he sure is. He's just now coming out of a meeting. Your timing was perfect. I'll put him on. We miss seeing you, Ned, take care."

"I miss you too." Ned could hear Susie announcing his name. Sheriff Cline got on the line right away.

"Well, good morning, Ned, to what do I owe this pleasure?" Not prone to small talk, the aggressive sheriff got right to the point.

Ned sat up in the lawn chair. "Well, I...uh have something I would like to discuss with you."

"Okay, fire away." Ned could hear him shuffling papers on his desk.

"Well, Sheriff...."

"It's Dave to you, Ned, please call me Dave."

Ned found the sheriff's plea for informality annoying. He knew the sheriff didn't care for him. It was just some BS from a big city career politician.

"Well, Dave, I've noticed some activity here in my

neighborhood in The Villages recently that has me a little concerned. Thought I would call and give you a heads up."

There was a short pause on the other end. "Hmm...., okay, but I can't say as I've heard of any problems in The Villages lately."

"Nothing has happened yet. It's a problem I see brewing."

"Okay, Ned, what is this problem you see brewing?"

"You know that Lex Higgins fella?"

The sheriff laughed, "My yes, who doesn't know him around here?"

"Well, I've noticed him driving around my neighborhood, Bridgeport, early in the morning a couple of times this week."

The sheriff nervously cleared his throat, he seemed slightly perturbed. "No crime against driving through a neighborhood. Maybe he's taking a little drive before work or something."

"That could be, Dave, and I wouldn't think much about it either, except he always pauses for awhile in front of the John Cullen house."

"Who's John Cullen?"

"A banker from Tampa."

The sheriff coughs up a couple of laughs, "Well, once again, my friend, there's certainly no law against pausing in front of somebody's house."

Feeling the sheriff's disdain, irritation rose in

Ned—the answer was intended to make him look foolish. Sheriff Cline knew the nature of the various neighborhoods in The Villages and he also knew it would be unusual for a young man of Lex Higgins' station in life to be frequenting a neighborhood like Bridgeport early in the morning.

The retired deputy composed himself and replied, choosing his words carefully. "We both know the story of Lex Higgins, Dave. He was a boy of much promise when he was in high school, but because of several set-backs in his life, he turned to a life of drugs and crime. We also know that he and Ali Brenneman were married for several years and that he was very distraught after his divorce from Ali. I believe my neighbor Cullen might be seeing Ali and that's why Lex is scoping out his house. It appears to me that Lex may feel threatened by Cullen."

"That's possible, I suppose. I was called to Cody's one night because of an altercation between Lex and some guy who had showed up there with his ex, but it wasn't much, nothing ever came of it."

Ned took a deep breath. "Dave, I was in law enforcement for many years and I have a pretty good feel for things—particularly when I know the people involved. The social and economic divide between Lex Higgins and John Cullen is enormous. It's one thing for Ali to date a local, but when she ties into someone as wealthy as Cullen, it's a whole different matter. Lex would feel helpless and inadequate in the face of the man like Cullen. And this Cullen fellow has a way about him; he's arrogant and showy."

"So Ali is dating Cullen?"

"Yes, I believe so. It's just a hunch, but I'm pretty sure I'm right and I think we could have a potential problem on our hands."

"With all due respect, Ned, I don't see much here. You have a young man who has driven around your village a couple of times, possibly to check out the area for a possible auto pick up. Then you conclude, without any real proof, that because the young man's former girlfriend is starting to see this Cullen fellow, that Lex Higgins has a vendetta against him. It's a real stretch, Ned. I can hardly spend our limited man hours chasing after something as hypothetical as this."

Ned exhaled slowly, trying to control his emotions. Not being able to see the potential for trouble here was bad police work, but the sheriff was the chief law enforcement official in the county and Ned was a nobody—a retired deputy with no real authority.

"Look, I don't care much for the guy, but something is happening here, Dave. I'm sorry you don't see it, but I believe it's real and could develop into something serious. I know you are busy, so I am not asking you to commit anyone directly to this situation, I just wanted to make you aware of the problem. If we work together, I think we can possibly avoid a serious problem. So if you don't mind I'm going to keep an eye on things."

The sheriff chuckled, "Okay, Ned, if you want to keep an eye on things and call the office once in a while, that's fine. You can leave the info with Susie."

Leave the info with Susie! Ned squeezed the arm of the chair; he didn't like being dismissed so offhandedly. He spoke slowly and quietly trying to control his emotions. "Sorry I took your time, Sheriff. I won't bother you again."

"No problem, Ned, always good to talk to you. I am running late, so I must be going. Have a great day, Ned."

Always respectful of the sheriff's position, a fuming Ned replied, "You too."

Ned was upset by the sheriff's reply, but it wasn't completely unexpected. The sheriff was used to a big city environment where crime was out of control and law enforcement spent the entire day trying to put out a maze of little fires. They didn't have time to anticipate or investigate a situation like the one with Lex Higgins. Ned understood this about the sheriff, but he didn't like it. The sheriff was no longer in the big city, and even though he was busy enough, he wasn't nearly as busy as he had been in Orlando.

Ned thought of several instances where he and former Sheriff Owen had thwarted a possible crime by being proactive and taking preemptive action before somebody got hurt. In his mind, to do anything less, no matter what your police background, was a sign of incompetence. He would keep an eye on Lex Higgins whether he got the support of the sheriff or not. And if push came to shove, he could enlist the support of his friends on the police department in nearby Wildwood. They didn't have any jurisdiction in The Villages, but they could put a bug in the new Sheriff's ear. Ned was certain that Sheriff Cline would cooperate.

"You okay out there?" Ned's wife, clad only in a pink terrycloth housecoat, stuck her head out of the sliding door. "You're usually on your second helping of oatmeal by now."

Ned smiled warmly, "Ah....just thinking about something, that's all."

"Well, breakfast is ready. Better get in here before it gets cold."

"Okay, dear." Ned dropped his phone in his pocket and hurried in the kitchen for his daily portion of hot oatmeal and wheat toast. After a quick breakfast, Ned would make a trip to the business district and visit Lex Higgins and Ali Brenneman at work. He hoped by talking them face to face that he might get a better feel for the situation.

Chapter 11

Lex drove slowly past the beautifully landscaped home looking for any sign of John Cullen. Lex knew what Cullen looked like, but for some unhealthy reason, he wanted to see him again. Unable to stop thinking about the man, Lex hoped that he might find him outside working in his yard or fiddling with one of the many toys that wealthy guys like Cullen kept in their garages. Several newspapers were scattered around his drive. It was obvious that Cullen wasn't home. Disappointed, he quickly looked around to see if anyone had been watching him. Satisfied that he had gone unnoticed, he did a quick U-turn and exited the neighborhood.

Ali had never dated a man as rich and powerful as John Cullen. A control freak by nature, the thought of losing Ali to a guy like him was driving Lex over the edge.

* * *

It was eight twenty-five when Lex turned left off 466 and sped into the employee parking lot. He quickly pulled to a stop in the only remaining parking spot. After some recent tardiness, he had assured his boss that he would never be late for work again. Mechanics such as Lex were supposed to be in the building at eight-thirty sharp. Eight-twenty nine was okay, but at eight-thirty one you could expect a tongue lashing from an angry boss. Lex killed the engine and hurried through the open garage door at the back of the building. Glancing at his watch, the time had just changed to eight-thirty at the exact moment when he passed under the garage door, the threshold for being considered inside of the building. His boss raised up from under the hood of a nearby vehicle, looked at his watch, held his stare on Lex briefly and then went back to work. Lex had dodged a bullet again.

Lex walked quickly to his work station, slid off his watch and Conference Championship ring from his high school basketball days and stuck them in a small drawer under his work bench. He lifted a couple of yellow work sheets off the bench placed there earlier in the morning by the office girl. He read over them quickly. She had scheduled him for a tune-up on a '65

Chevy and the repair of a water pump on a 2002 Ford pickup. He decided to do the tune-up first.

Lex reached under the bench, lifted up his heavy toolbox and dropped it on the scarred oak bench top. As Lex prepared to start to work for the day, images of Ali and Cullen raced through his mind. Even when he was busy, Ali was never far from his thoughts. Working on cars was like falling off a log for Lex, which allowed him to worry and work at the same time. Images of the two of them cuddled together and looking at travel brochures to exotic locations would often flash through his mind. Sometimes his thoughts would become so intense that he would cramp up and become physically ill. An occasional race to the bathroom was not unusual for Lex.

During his marriage to Ali, the majority of their arguments centered around their lack of money. Her main concern was that she didn't want to bring children into the world until they made enough money to give them a safe and secure future. A man like Cullen could give Ali all the financial security she needed—this made Lex feel small and worthless. It made him feel like a failure.

But there was a glimmer of hope in the midst of all of this worry. Lex clung desperately to the belief that if given enough time, he could get Ali back. If she could only stay single for another year or so, Lex would have enough time to complete his plan to buy his first Jiffy Lube—something he had always dreamed of doing. With the first one in hand, he could then expand and buy several more franchises. Then he would have enough money to buy a house on Lake Harris and give Ali the financial security she needed. They would start dating again, fall in love, remarry, and live happily ever after. All he needed was time, just a year or so.

The only thing standing in his way was John Cullen. If he stole Ali away from him and married her, all plans were off. His only hope for any kind of happiness would be snatched away from him. In his eyes, Cullen was the devil, the man who was trying to keep him from having the thing he wanted most out of life—Ali Brenneman.

Chapter 12

Ned's 1998 brown pickup rolled to a stop in the front lot at Tire Hut. Glancing through the always open garage doors, he saw Lex Higgins working on a vehicle in the bay nearest to the front office. Ned purposely parked on the north side of the large parking lot so he would have to walk past Lex's work station on his way to the front door. The door to the old truck creaked open and Ned slid out of the front seat.

As Ned approached Lex's work area, he was shocked by the appearance of the young man he saw leaning against the front fender of a classic old Chevy adjusting a wrench. The thin, gaunt looking young man was a far cry from the outstanding athlete who gave the local fans so many great moments as the star of the Belleview High School basketball team several years ago. One look at him and Ned could see that life had not been good to Lex Higgins. Pausing near the front of the truck, Ned spoke to the former star athlete, "Mornin', Lex."

Surprised, Lex paused before starting his descent back under the hood.

"Well...uh, hi, Mr. Carpenter." He snatched a work rag from his back pocket and began wiping his hands.

Ned raised his hand slightly, "Oh please, don't clean up, I just wanted to say hello."

Lex ignored his plea and continued to wipe his hands. Finally, he stuffed the rag back in his pocket and walked toward Ned with his hand extended. "Good to see you, sir. Bringing in your truck, I see."

The two men shook hands. "Yes, I...uh brought my brown beauty in to see about getting the oil changed."

Lex smiled at the brown beauty comment. "We're pretty much booked-up today, but Shelley might be able to work you in soon."

Appearing to be embarrassed by his appearance, Lex nervously yanked the rag out of his back pocket and began cleaning his hands again.

"Ok, thanks, maybe she can work me in tomorrow morning. I believe you are open on Saturday morning, aren't you?"

"Yes, we sure are." Lex's eyes looked anxious as if he somehow suspected that Ned's visit was not an accident.

Ned noticed his apprehension and replied, "Just saw you working here and thought I would say hi to the best Cub Scout I ever had in Pack 24."

Lex's face flushed red at the nice comment about his days as a Cub Scout. "You were a good leader, Mr. Carpenter."

Ned smiled. "Still got that Firebird?"

"Oh yeah, sure do." Lex showed a prideful grin.

Ned's brow lifted just a little. "I was out fishing today and I believe I saw your Firebird cruising around my neighborhood."

The grin vanished from Lex's face; he was obviously shaken by the remark. It was just the reaction Ned was looking for.

"Uh...yeah, that was me alright. We...uh got a pick-up there later today and I was locating the house."

Unable to hold eye contact, Lex looked away from Ned.

"Anybody I know?"

"Ah, no, no, just some rich Villager who wants his car serviced before he gets here tomorrow. I'm sure you wouldn't know him." Lex shook his head uneasily as if agreeing with his own statement and hoping Ned would too.

Ned backed off, wanting to keep the conversation light and casual. "You're right, Lex, I've only met a few of my neighbors."

Lex once again extended his right hand for a shake. "I'd better get back to work, don't want to get on the bad side of the new boss. Nice talking with you, Mr. Carpenter."

Ned shook Lex's outstretched hand and smiled warmly, "Tell your mom hi for me, will ya?"

"Sure thing, Mr. Carpenter."

"Great talking to you, Lex!"

"Same here." Lex hurried back to the front of the truck, grabbed his wrench off the front fender and ducked under the hood.

Ned stepped through the front door and walked toward the service desk. He had found out what he wanted to know. Lex's reaction when he mentioned seeing his car at Bridgeport spoke volumes. Also, during a brief conversation with Cullen at the Bridgeport mail drop, Cullen told Ned that he always had his vehicles serviced by the original dealer and that he would never trust them to a local garage. He was almost certain now that his hunch about Lex and Cullen was correct. Things were starting to add up, but Ned needed to make one more visit before he could feel one hundred percent certain that he was on the right track.

* * *

Lex yanked hard on the wrench to loosen the spark plug on the big V-8. He stood and dropped the dirty plug on the nearby service cart. Busy working again, he couldn't stop thinking about the visit from

Ned Carpenter. Was it just a friendly visit or was he suspicious about something? Lex's criminal past made him nervous around law enforcement types, even an old family friend. Did Ned Carpenter know something about his involvement with Rudy and the meth labs? Did he somehow know how much he disliked Cullen? Lex paused and thought for a minute. He shook his head—there's no way Ned could know about his association with Rudy. He hadn't told anyone and Rudy was a pro, he wouldn't tell a soul either. It was highly unlikely that Ned Carpenter would know anything about his connection to John Cullen, and his explanation for being in Ned's village that morning was very plausible. And besides, Ned was retired now and living the good life. Why would he care what's going on with little ole' Lex Higgins. Breathing a sigh of relief, he ducked back under the hood.

* * *

The old truck groaned to a stop in front of CVS, followed by a loud backfire. Slightly embarrassed, Ned exited the truck and hustled inside the store. Once inside, he looked around for Ali. He didn't see her anywhere around the front of the store, so he headed for the back. After walking a short distance, he heard her distinctive laugh coming from the back of the store near the pharmacy.

When he reached the pharmacy, he saw her standing and talking to another employee. Pretending to be shopping for a pain killer, he stopped a few feet from Ali and lifted a bottle of Aleve off the shelf. Fortunately, her conversation soon broke up and she turned and started down the aisle toward him. Her face instantly broke into a broad smile when she saw him reading the instructions on the bottle.

"Why hello, Mr. Carpenter! It's so nice to see you!"

Ned carefully set the unwanted bottle of Aleve back on the shelf and turned toward her. A smile spread across his weathered face, "Oh my goodness, Ali, how are you?"

Ali smiled shyly and replied. "I'm fine, thank you, and how is Molly doing? I haven't talked to her for quite a while."

"Good, still up in Gainesville and running the kids all over the place."

"Tell her to give me a call the next time she's in town, maybe we can get together."

Ned smiled, "Sure will, Ali, I know she'd like that. How are things with you? I'm surprised some lucky guy hasn't snatched you up by now. You're as pretty as ever."

Ali blushed. "Oh, I'm kind of dating a guy, nothing serious."

"Anybody I know?"

"I don't think so. He's a banker from Tampa, so

you probably don't know him."

"Try me, I know 'bout everybody around here." Ned was pushing the conversation harder than he normally would, but he was certain that Ali wouldn't think much about it. He had known her all of her life and she trusted him.

"His name is John Cullen."

Ned smiled broadly. "You underestimated old Ned, I not only know him, he's my neighbor in Bridgeport."

"Oh my, what a small world! Mom told me that you had moved to The Villages. How do you like it?"

"Love it."

Ali gave a quick nod of the head and then changed the subject. "Does Molly still have the same phone number? I may give her a call."

"No, they moved into a bigger place last fall and she had to change her home phone number. I have it at home. I'll call you this week and let you know what her new number is."

Ned was pleased that Ali had asked about his daughter's phone number, it gave him another reason to keep in contact with her. The final pieces of the puzzle were falling into place and he was absolutely certain that he was on the right track.

"Thanks, Mr. Carpenter, I would love to catch up on things with her."

"No problem at all, Ali."

"Well, I'd better get back to work. I have a lot to

do."

"Oh, sure, it was great seeing you, Ali. Take care."

"Good-bye, Mr. Carpenter," she smiled warmly and hurried off.

Ned grabbed an inexpensive box of the CVS brand pain killers and headed for the nearest checkout counter.

Chapter 13

John pressed hard on the accelerator. The tires squealed, the sleek auto raced up to seventy, then eighty. His hair blew helter-skelter in the hot August wind. Earlier that morning, he had decided to drive his prized Mercedes Roadster to his Village house for the weekend to hopefully impress Ali. She had seen his big house in The Villages and his new Escalade, but she had never seen his expensive sports car. It was all part of his plan to impress her with his wealth and stature as a way of possibly luring her into the bedroom.

He lifted his iPhone from its holder on the center console and punched in Ali's number. The loud music on the radio went quiet as the Bluetooth connection took over the speakers. John eased off the big engine and slowed down to reduce the wind noises.

"Hello, John, is that you?"

"Yes, can you hear me alright? I'm in my convertible."

"There is some wind noise, but I can hear you okay."

"Oh good, I can usually hear okay with the top down, but I never know how my Mercedes Roadster is going to treat me, depends on the wind."

John felt sophomoric mentioning the make of his car, but he couldn't resist. This girl had him back on his heels and he was anxious to try and impress her.

There was a deafening pause on the other end and then Ali replied, not mentioning his Mercedes, "Where are you? I thought you would be at your company golf outing."

Her failure to mention his car didn't go unnoticed by John. It was another indication that she was more mature and self-confident than the other girls he had dated, and he didn't like it. He liked having the upper hand and with this girl it seemed to be the other way around.

Feeling somewhat diminished, he responded, "Well, some of the guys couldn't make it and others were having to do a lot of schedule juggling, so we decided to delay the outing until later in the summer."

John squirmed in his seat. The truth was that he had called the outing off himself, explaining to his golfing friends that he was too involved in a large merger deal to take that much time off. He had sent them all an e-mail declaring, "We're down to the wire and my phone is ringing off the hook." But in reality, his phone had only rung once that weekend regarding the merger.

"Oh, I'm so sorry your outing is off. I'll bet you're disappointed," Ali said sincerely.

"Yea, I really look forward to it, but we'll get it done later in the summer—so it's no biggee."

"Well, that's good." Ali didn't say anymore and John knew that she was waiting on an explanation for his call. He was a little reticent and embarrassed to tell her that he was on his way up to The Villages. He wasn't sure she wanted to see him as badly as he wanted to see her.

"Well...uh you'll never guess where I'm headed right now."

"To the ocean?"

"No, no I'm...uh actually on 75 heading up to The Villages. Can you believe it?"

"Well no, that's a surprise."

John felt warm under his arms, "Yea, I had some things to do up there, so I thought I'd better head on up."

Ali replied quickly, "Sounds like you'll be busy."

John was rattled by the nonchalant response from Ali. His pride wouldn't let him tell her that his only reason for coming was to try and see her. He thought for a moment and then replied, "Oh I have some things to go over with my landscaper, but I certainly won't be tied up the whole weekend."

"Well, I'm glad someone will have some free time, I sure won't. I didn't have anything going on so I volunteered to work today."

"Really?" John was gravely disappointed. This was totally unexpected.

"Yes, and Sunday I told mom I would help her stain her deck. It's really in bad shape."

John's heart sank. He had to think of some way to see her. He pondered the situation for a moment and then humbly replied, "Would you consider doing something after work possibly? After all, it is Saturday. We could do something relaxing, like cook out at my place and enjoy the lovely sunset over the golf course. It's spectacular."

"Oh, I would love to, John, but I have to work until ten tonight. Two girls called in sick and they're shorthanded, so I volunteered to work until closing time."

John didn't give up. "Why don't I help you and your mom stain that deck on Sunday. I love staining." This was another lie; John had never stained anything in his life.

Ali's voice was almost inaudible, "Staining mom's deck has never been one of my favorite things to do. Maybe I could...."

"What time are you starting? I could be there first

thing Sunday morning."

There was another pause. John had stuck his neck out and he was waiting to see if she would chop it off.

"Well...uh, we were planning on starting around nine o'clock. I suppose that might work"

"One of my golfing groups is having its annual cocktail party later on Sunday afternoon."

"Oh my, I would hate to take you away from your party. I wouldn't feel right about that."

"Oh no, no, can you go to the party with me? It starts at four and lasts well into the evening. We could do your mom's deck and then stop by the party for a couple of drinks. You could meet some of my friends. How about it?"

"I think I might feel out of place with all those wealthy people and all. Are you sure?'

John could sense that Ali was curious about the party, so he pushed on. "Are you kidding? You will be the prettiest girl at the party! I'm sure my golfing buddies will be all over you."

She laughter nervously, "Well, I doubt that."

John was feeling more confident. "Okay, babe, looks like we've got a date. I'll be over at your mom's at nine and we'll knock that deck out and then head over to my friend's house later that afternoon for a drink."

"After I freshin' up."

"Oh, certainly."

John glanced in his mirror—a sleek Corvette was

pushing in on him and looked like it might try to pass.

"Well, it's not what I thought I would be doing Sunday, but okay, it's a date!"

"Great, see you at nine sharp on Sunday morning."

"Okay, good-bye, John."

"Bye."

The Vet pulled alongside him. The young man behind the wheel grinned and gave him a thumbs up. John, buoyed by his Sunday date with Ali pushed hard on the accelerator. The car surged to over a hundred miles an hour in just a couple of seconds. The Vet grew smaller and smaller in his rear view mirror. John raced up to a hundred and forty and then backed off not wanting to chance a speeding ticket. A big smile spread across his face, his huge ego had been mollified once again, if only temporarily.

Chapter 14

It was 12:30 p.m, half an hour past closing time and Lex was just climbing into the front seat of his Firebird. He had worked over to gain some badly needed brownie points with the new boss. Suddenly his phone started to ring. Rudy's name popped up on the screen. He lifted the phone from the console and answered.

"Yeah, Rudy, what's up?"

"Did I wait long enough? Are you off work?"

"Yeah, I just got off."

There was a pause, it sounded like Rudy was taking a drag on weed. "There's no way in hell I'm going to give you twenty-five per cent."

"Don't do blow on the phone, Rudy, okay?"

"My, aren't we the sensitive one?"

"If you don't do twenty-five, it's no deal, I'm out."

Lex put the car in gear and started backing up.

"Not so fast there, Mr. Over-reactor. I will go twenty percent with a five percent bonus if you increase our business significantly."

"Significantly? What the hell does that mean?"

"Double."

"Double?" Lex shook his head and glanced out the driver's side window. "That's impossible."

"It's different now, Lex, things are different. There's a lot more users out there than there were a few years ago. People are down on their luck, and the ones who have jobs are being asked to work longer and longer hours. That's why they're using crank, it helps them get through their long work days. They buy the shit from us on the weekend and then they suck on a plastic bottle every morning so they can work sixteen hours in some shithole. This economy is making things very tough on the working class folks. There are crank users all over the fucking place."

Rudy's explanation hit Lex like a ton of bricks. A bolt of sadness shot through him. "Poor bastards," he mumbled.

"I know, and they need us more than ever now."

Lex glanced down at the Championship ring on his grease stained finger. Visions of scoring the winning basket in the final game of the sectional tournament flashed through his mind. He remembered how everybody had surrounded him, jumping up and down and patting him on the back.

What a hero he had been to so many people. And now, years later, he was talking to a lowlife like Rudy about selling meth to poor, downtrodden folks to help them get through the day. How far he had fallen since those glory days back in high school. His life was at rock bottom now; nobody was patting him on the back and cheering him on. A divorced ex-con, he was broke and down on his luck and Rudy knew it. Rudy was playing on his vulnerabilities, dangling the possibility of making lots of money in front of him. It was obvious what Rudy was doing, but he was right, Lex was broke and needed cash. *Damn him!* He thought. Then he shook his head and replied, "Okay, asshole, I'm in. What's next?"

"Great! It's good to have you back, my friend. It's the weekend, ya know, so we're cooking away out here. Why don't you come on out and look things over. You can start tomorrow."

"Okay, how do I get there?"

"Just take 301 north and then turn right at the first road north of 484. Drive about five miles past the old Hanson horse farm and there's a little dirt road on the left just a few hundred yards on down the road. It's hard to see, so look carefully."

"I'm going to grab a burger, I'll be there in about twenty minutes."

"You're in the red Firebird I take it?"

"Of course."

"Okay, see you in a little while."

"10-4."

Lex started up, made his way onto 466. McDonald's was just ahead. A few seconds later, he turned into the drive-thru. He was lucky. For a Saturday around noon, there were only a few cars in line. He entered toward the now open drive-thru speaker and ordered a double cheeseburger. A short time later, with the warm burger in his hand, he exited the McDonald's parking lot and continued on his trip to meet Rudy.

Lex was deeply conflicted as he drove up the highway toward his rendezvous with Rudy. Joining forces with Rudy was very risky, but what options did he have? His life was going nowhere and he could barely make his court payments for the damage to his former condo each month. He was always broke and more than anything, he knew he would never be able to give Ali the life she deserved on the pathetic income he was earning now. If he started selling meth again, he could save up enough money to start his first Jiffy Lube. Hopefully it would do well and then he would be in a position to open several more. Soon he would be a wealthy man. It was a big gamble to start cooking again, but it would allow him the opportunity to pursue his dream. One thing was for sure, if he screwed up, he would go back to prison for a long time.

Lex took the last bite of his cheeseburger and washed it down with the remnants in a day old bottled water sitting in his console. He turned right at the first road north of 484 and drove for a while. After passing the abandoned horse farm, he began searching the thick weeds alongside the road for the little lane that led to the meth lab. Soon, an opening appeared. Two well grooved lanes led up through an overgrown pasture. Checking his rearview mirror to be certain no one was around, he turned onto the narrow road.

Assorted loose change, lip balm, a Bic lighter, and a few nuts and bolts, rattled in the console as he drove slowly down the rutted path. About fifty yards later, he took a sharp right into a large gravel lot. The Firebird came to a stop in front of an old rickety farmhouse with a detached garage. Both buildings looked like they were ready to collapse. Weeds were protruding from the gutter on the garage and the paint was peeling off the entire surface of the wood-frame building. The old farmhouse wasn't faring much better with its sagging gutters and faded aluminum siding. Several pickups, along with Rudy's Harley were parked haphazardly in the gravel area near Lex's Firebird.

Lex climbed out of his car. He could hear country and western music coming from the inside of the large barn-like garage. An odor reminiscent of rotten eggs permeated the outside air contaminating everything it touched, including the ground outside the windows. Lex paused, *it's a dirty business,* he thought. He shook his head and started toward the garage, only to be greeted by a smiling Rudy as he approached the front door.

"Hey, Lex! I've been waiting on you."

"Hi, Rudy."

"Come on in, let me show you what we got cookin' here," Rudy laughed sarcastically.

Lex nodded and followed Rudy through the open door.

"I had forgotten how strong the smell is," Lex growled.

"Ah! You'll get used to it. Besides, we all smell the same, so we don't notice it. That's nothing new, is it?"

"No, I guess not." Lex said quietly. But actually, he had forgotten about the smells. He was younger then and so intent upon making some money that he didn't think much about all of the trips to Walmart to buy cheap t-shirts and jeans. The odor was so pungent that it was almost impossible to wash the stench away. You might get by with a wash or two, but basically you had to change clothes after a few bouts of cooking. Some guys didn't and they walked around smelling like rotten eggs all the time—a dead give-away to anyone who knew anything about meth.

Once inside the old building, Lex took a look around. There were four thirty-something men and women in badly worn jeans and t-shirts milling around the barn busily tending to their respective jobs. In the center of the room, on the badly cracked cement floor, sat two long sagging aluminum tables. The tables were covered by the many chemicals and apparatus used in the rather complex process of cooking meth. Cans of kerosene, large plastic pop bottles, small packages containing red phosphorous, hydriodic acid, lye, and other chemicals were lined up on the table tops. One of the men was about to pour crystallized hydrochloride salt through a cloth filter into a small container—the final step before allowing the salt to dry into methamphetamine.

The man looked up at Lex and smiled. Lex recognized the slender man from his previous experiences in meth labs in the Lake County area. He was shocked by the man's appearance. His dark eyes, blackened teeth and frail body were all tell-tell signs of a serious meth user. Meth not only sucks all of the dopamine from your brain, the chemical that creates pleasure, but it also ruins your teeth and keeps you awake at night—hence the black teeth and darkened eyes. These workers were a sad lot, that's for sure. What kind of life must you have to end up working for eight bucks an hour in a meth lab, in a dark, dirty place fraught with danger? In the ocean of life, these folks were the bottom dwellers, the losers in life who had long since given up any hope of realizing the American Dream.

A bolt of fear shot up Lex's spine as he stood next to Rudy and surveyed the dirty little meth factory. What a dark, dismal place this was, both depressing and sad.

What am I doing here? Lex thought. He was ready to turn and run, to tell Rudy to find himself another fool who would risk everything to make a few bucks, but he realized that the sad looking man at the end of the table looked very much like him. In many ways, his life was miserable also. He felt hopeless and depressed most of the time and his physical appearance, absent the bad teeth, was very much like the slender man. But there was a difference between him and the slender man—a very big difference. While the meth had sucked the joy out of the man's life, it could not do that to Lex. For all his problems, Lex had always been smart enough to see the enormous downside of using meth. He had been able to shoulder off all attempts at getting him hooked on crank. "I won't do it because it 'ruins your brain'," he would so often say. His past problems had involved prescription drugs, pot, and alcohol, but never meth.

Struggling to keep his wits about him, Lex fought to keep his mind on subject. There were huge risks in what he was about to do and he knew it, but there was also a huge upside. He could use this operation to get the cash he needed to become an entrepreneur, to own his own business and to buy those Jiffy Lubes he had so often dreamed about. Then Ali would see his successes and take him back. They would build a life together right here in central Florida and live happily ever after. He was intoxicated by the thought of it. It blinded him to the realities of what he was about to do.

Lex felt a bump on his arm, "Hey, Lex, you daydreamin'?"

"No, just thinking about something."

Rudy grinned, "I know this ain't the Hilton or anything, but its money in the bank, buddy, money in the bank!"

"I know, I know."

"Well, what do you think?"

Lex shook his head, his eyes narrowed. He pointed across the room at two five gallon gas cans sitting on the floor near the two tables. "Why do you leave those lids off the kerosene, Rudy? That stuff evaporates faster than gasoline. This room is full of fumes, it could blow up at any time."

"Put the lids on the kerosene," Rudy barked at one of the ladies.

A skinny lady with dirty blond hair wearing a New York Yankee's ball cap, hurried over and started to put the caps on the two cans of kerosene. "This one's almost empty," she shouted.

"It doesn't matter," Lex ordered. "Keep the fucking lids on at all times! And while you're at it, open both windows so we can get a cross breeze in here. I can't believe this dump hasn't blown up already."

Appearing annoyed by a stranger barking orders at her, the lady nonetheless quickly navigated the room, opening the single windows on either side of the building.

Undeterred, Lex moved nearer the two tables peppering the workers with questions. It was obvious that the boss was back in town. An honor student in high school, Lex was the smartest guy in the room and it didn't take long for everyone to realize it.

After a few minutes, Lex stepped back from the others and barked, "Do what I say and everybody will make more money. And, here's the good part, if we make more money, you will all get a piece of the action."

Lex felt a tug on his shirt. A clearly aggravated Rudy leaned forward and whispered in his ear. "What the hell are you talking about? I can't pay them any bonus or anything."

Lex leaned toward Rudy and whispered, "At the end of the month we'll give them each fifty bucks or something. We'll never miss it and they will be thrilled to death. It will keep them motivated and give them a reason to work harder. We need these folks. There's not a whole shitload of people out there who want to work in this hell hole and risk going to jail. Use your head, Rudy."

Rudy's eyes narrowed, his left eye twitched, a nervous reaction when he was angry. "Okay, Lex, but we better make more money or your ass is grass."

A confident grin spread across Lex's face. "Don't worry, Rudy, you'll get your money. When I'm done with this operation, we will be making better meth so we will be able to thin it out and get more product. Our profits will sky rocket."

"They'd better." Rudy's glare was dark and nasty, the glare of a bad man who had grown to enjoy peddling poison to hopeless people. Lex was caught off balance by the intensity of the stare. He had known Rudy a long time and had little respect for him, but that was the look of a dangerous man, a man devoid of feeling.

Chapter 15

John's left turn signal blinked. He gunned it and turned onto Buena Vista Boulevard, one of the two main arteries in The Villages. Once on the beautiful boulevard, John accelerated hard again, trying to impress anyone who could see him in his flashy convertible. Soon he was up to sixty miles an hour, well over the thirty-five speed limit. Approaching the first roundabout to Lake Sumter Landing, the nearest town square to John's village, he eased off the powerful engine and skirted around the well landscaped roundabout. He negotiated several more roundabouts, finally arriving at 466A a few minutes later. He turned left on 466A and started the last leg of his journey to Ali's mother's house in Fruitland Park, a small town adjacent to The Villages.

It was a few minutes before nine o'clock on this

warm Sunday morning and the bright sun was starting to rise in the eastern sky above the many palm trees that bordered the busy roadway. It was indeed a lovely sight and John was in a very good mood. He was excited about seeing the lovely Ali again, but he was even more excited about taking her to the cocktail party and showing her off to his golfing buddies. He would be the man of the hour with a lady as young and beautiful as Ali on his arm. That is if he lived through this staining job. A successful banker, it had been years since he had done manual labor of any kind. "Why bust your butt, when you can hire someone to do it for you?" he would often chortle to his golfing buddies.

A short time later, he flipped on his left turn signal, slowed and turned onto Rose Avenue. He drove slowly down the bumpy road, searching the name plates that bordered the driveways along the street looking for the name of Sally Brenneman. Ali told John that her mother's house was about half-way down the street. Unlike the more upscale Villages, these homes were primarily small ranch homes and doublewides.

"This is about what I expected," John grunted sarcastically. Up ahead, John spotted Ali's green Honda Civic parked in the driveway of a house.

John turned in and parked behind Ali's Civic and killed the engine. He was surprised by the neat condition of the yard and house, It was evident that

Mrs. Brenneman took great pride in her modest ranch home. John felt nervous. There was always a slight uncertainty in the air when he was around Ali, an unintended tension that kept him back on his heels. He stepped out of his car and made his way up to the front door. Most of the women John had dated since his divorce were overexcited to see him and would come running out to greet him—bouncing down the front sidewalk in their skimpy halter tops and tight shorts. With Ali, he would not get his usual greeting. The front of the house was stone quiet. *These nice girls are a pain in the ass,* he thought as he pushed the front door bell.

John waited for a few seconds, but no one came. He looked down at his watch; it was about five after nine. He certainly wasn't early, and while he didn't expect Ali to do flip-flops over him, he had hoped that she would have at least some minor interest in his arrival. He hit the doorbell again. He could hear it ringing inside. John was starting to get a little perturbed. He bent down and peered through the beveled glass door. It was a little blurry, but he could see images out in the backyard, probably around the deck, and he could also hear an occasional burst of laughter. But John wasn't laughing. He was getting more and more upset by the minute. His plan had been to exchange niceties at the door and pause while they went goo-goo over his beautiful Mercedes Roadster. Then, as was his custom, he would lead them to his car and show them all the impressive and unheard of features on the ultra-expensive auto. Much to John's disappointment, that wasn't happening today. Ali and her mother didn't seem to be the least bit interested in his arrival and he was becoming more agitated. He angrily punched the doorbell button with his knuckle, but once again, no one came.

Beside himself, John decided to march to the back of the house and give these ladies a piece of his mind. His face flush with anger, he hopped off the porch and walked determinedly toward the back, brushing aside the feathery leaves of a large fern on his way. Pretty or not, he wasn't going to tolerate this kind of treatment from some low level clerk at a drugstore. He rounded the last corner of the house and before he could say anything, he stopped dead in his tracks. There she was, standing next to the deck, holding a small paint brush in her right hand and laughing like crazy. She was wearing a red bandanna, a little white t-shirt, very snug faded jeans and pair of old tennis shoes. But even dressed down, she still looked absolutely gorgeous. Her mother, busy painting the floor on the deck, caught a glimpse of John rounding the corner.

"Uh...honey, your friend is here," she said as she stood and flashed John a big smile. John was surprised by how pretty her mother was. A few pounds heavier than Ali and of our course much older, but otherwise she looked very much like Ali. Ali's mom was an exceptionally attractive middle-aged woman.

Ali turned around and smiled broadly at John. She must have noticed the expression on John's face and quickly blurted, "Oh my goodness, I'm so sorry, John, is it nine o'clock already?"

"Why...uh yes, it's almost a quarter after and I've been standing out front ringing the doorbell for several minutes now."

"Oh John, I'm so sorry! How rude of me, please forgive me." She laid her brush on top of the paint can and hurried over next to him. No hug or anything, but he still enjoyed having her next to him.

"Please come and meet my mom," she said. She slid her hand under John's arm and gently pulled him toward her mother.

Once again, the anger he'd felt melted into a mellow twilight zone of contentment. He had gone from total indignation to a sense of complete submissiveness within a few seconds. These feelings were so unlike him that he couldn't believe what was happening. Once again, he found himself having an out-of-body experience just by being in the very presence of this lovely creature.

Her mom stepped over to the railing on the large deck and extended her hand to him. "Why, hello John, how nice to meet you."

"The pleasure is all mine," he replied.

"I've heard a lot about you."

"Mom!" a slightly embarrassed Ali shouted.

Her mom smiled sheepishly and went on, "We only pay minimum wage, ya' know."

John laughed heartedly, smitten by her cordiality. "That will be fine, thanks." John replied.

"And let me add my apology for not greeting you at the door. We got to laughing and didn't hear the bell. I had no idea it was past nine."

"No problem, Mrs. Brenneman, no problem at all."

"Sally, please call me Sally. I mean we are about the same age, you know.

"Mom!" Ali shrieked even louder than the first time.

John laughed nervously, "Close enough, I guess."

Sally shook her head.

Walking over to the side of the deck, Ali lifted a bucket of stain and returned back to John.

"Here ya go, John. We best get going, I don't want to miss that get-together this afternoon."

"I agree," John replied quickly. "Where do I begin?"

"Well, we thought you could do the railings while mom and I worked on the floor and the stairs."

"Sounds like a plan," John said as he stepped over to the deck and began to paint the front railing. The deck was much larger than he expected, so John knew that they would have to hustle to get it done. But get it done he would. He wasn't going to miss his chance to show his beautiful new love interest to his golfing buddies —not for the world.

Chapter 16

Lex had taken a huge gamble earlier in the day when he called Ali's mom in an attempt to get Ali's new phone number. Ali had changed her number recently to prevent Lex from calling her, but he wanted to reach her and tell her about his future plans of becoming the owner of several Jiffy Lubes in the central Florida area. He felt it was important for her to know that he too had a future and that he was not just some loser working in a garage.

Sally Brenneman, who always had a soft spot for Lex, explained that Ali was at a cookout at the Village of Pennecamp with a friend. Lex concluded that the friend must be Cullen. Ali didn't know anyone else in The Villages well enough to be invited to a cookout, so this had to be at the home of one of Cullen's rich buddies. Lex asked for her new number explaining that he had some good news for Ali. Her mother, unable to hurt the young man who had been such a big part of their lives for so many years, very reluctantly gave him the new number. He thanked her and hung up and hurriedly added the number to his speed dial.

Feeling more and more threatened by this man who could offer Ali so much, Lex decided to go to Pennecamp and see for himself what Ali was up to. He knew it was the wrong thing to do, but at this point, Lex was not thinking rationally. He had to see what was going on at this party. Was she walking around some beautiful pool area and hanging on this guy's arm? Was she giggling and rubbing up next to him and acting amorously toward him in front of his rich buddies? His fantasies were running wild and his rage was mounting.

A few minutes later, he pulled into the Village of Pennecamp and started driving around looking for signs of a get-together—a large number of golf carts and or automobiles parked out in front of a house. It didn't take long to find the party. He rounded a corner and saw several golf carts, along with Lexus's, BMW's, Cadillac's, and other expensive automobiles parked in front of a large lavish home. He gunned it a little and darted toward the house. As he got closer, he eased off the accelerator, not wanting to draw attention to his car. While navigating his way through the bunched up vehicles, he glanced at the front of the sprawling residence, but saw no activity. Luckily, the house was on a corner lot. When he rounded the corner he could her voices and laughter coming from the backyard.

Surrounding the pool at the back of the house was a large contingent of casually dressed Villagers, drinking, eating and talking loudly. Lex had found the party. It didn't take him long to pick Ali out of the group. Her long brown hair stood out like a sore thumb among the aging, mostly white-haired folks at the party. Much to his delight, she didn't appear to be talking with Cullen. She was standing near the hot tub and talking to an elderly man and his wife. He had only seen Cullen once at the shop, but he was certain that the man Ali was talking to wasn't him. Across the pool, a man who looked like Cullen was standing and talking to another gentleman. Lex looked closer. "That's him," he grunted. Lex felt a little better knowing that Ali wasn't hanging all over the guy. His deepest fears had been alleviated—if only momentarily.

With his insecurities still bubbling over, he decided to take another lap around the block and get one more look at Ali. He felt confident that the people at the party were busy talking and had not noticed his car. He hastily drove around the block and turned the corner at the big house for one last look. Ali was still standing and talking to the same couple. Cullen was still across the pool. Lex breathed a sigh of relief and decided he had taken enough risks and headed for home.

Barely out of view of the house, he gently lifted a joint out of his console, stuck it in his mouth and lit up. At the same time, his cell phone began to ring— Ali's picture was on the screen. At first he didn't want to answer, but curiosity got the best of him and he touched the screen and answered. She was incensed. She saw his car go by, more than likely the second time, and she was not happy. Surprised by the call and feeling flustered, Lex struggled to come up with a reason for being in Pennecamp.

He hesitated for a minute and then blurted out, "I was looking for a buddy of mine who's putting in a new countertop and owes me some money, that's all, calm down."

"I don't believe you, Lex. I think you're spying on me and I don't like it one bit!"

Lex shot back, "You're crazy, I'm not spying on you! I couldn't care less about you and your pansy-ass boyfriend! I've got my own life to lead!"

Ali's voice softened a little, "I hope you do, Lex, because I also have a life to lead and I don't want you interfering. If you keep it up, I may have to consider getting a restraining order."

Lex's temper flared. "Don't flatter yourself, Ali, there's no one harassing you! I was just out there looking for a friend who owes me some money. And you can get all the restraining orders you want, I don't give a damn!"

"I'm serious about this, Lex, I really am. Stay out of my life!" With that, the phone went dead on the other end.

Lex stared at the screen for a moment and then tossed his iPhone furiously toward the passenger seat. It banged against the door and fell harmlessly to the middle of the empty seat. Lex was beside himself. *She can't tell me what to do!*

He slammed down on the accelerator, his Firebird shot down Buena Vista Boulevard toward 466A. He glanced down at the speedometer, he was doing sixty. The speed limit on Buena Vista was thirty-five. Lex knew that The Villages did not have an official police force, but they did have a Community Watch, a large contingent of mainly retired law enforcement officials who patrolled The Villages 24-7 in little pickup trucks. And while they couldn't arrest anyone, they could take his license number and report the incident to the county cops. One thing Lex didn't need right now was any grief from the cops, so he eased off the gas and slowed to about thirty-five. He took another drag, but even the mellowing effect of the joint couldn't overcome his anger towards Cullen. "If it weren't for Cullen, Ali would be more open to seeing me," he seethed.

Lex exited onto 466A, his bloodshot eyes scanned the road ahead. He took another hard drag on the joint holding the hot smoke deep inside his lungs for as long as he could. He exhaled slowly. His eyes fluttered from the sting of the acidic smoke. An anxious feeling came over him as he tried to make sense of things. His big problem still remained— Cullen. This arrogant rich guy was trying to take away his last opportunity for true happiness.

A feeling of desperation was rising inside him as he struggled to keep control of his emotions. He shook his head violently and then let out a guttural laugh and mumbled, "You'r dead meat, Mr. Hot Shot—dead meat!"

Chapter 17

Ali pushed her phone into her purse, took a deep breath and tried to compose herself. She paused, exhaled, and walked back to the pool area. Stepping past the open sliders, she fluffed her hair and looked for the people she had been talking with when Lex drove past.

"Hey, good looking!"

Ali felt a hand on her left arm. She spun around. "Oh, hi, John."

"Everything okay? You looked a little serious in there for a second."

"Oh yes, I'm fine, just a stop at the ladies' room and a quick phone call, that's all." She smiled warmly, not wanting her personal problems to affect the party and more importantly, her relationship with John.

"Having a good time?"

"Oh yes, I'm having a wonderful time, everyone has made me feel so welcome. Thank you so much for inviting me to come and meet all your friends, they are so nice!"

A smug smile spread across John's face. "Yes, these folks are the best."

Ali nodded in agreement.

"Nice party, but the hors d'oeuvres aren't filling me up. I'm a little hungry. How about you?"

Actually, Ali wasn't very hungry. She was a light eater by nature, but with the drive-by incident fresh in her mind, she was ready for a change of scenery. "Yes, I could use a bite. What do you have in mind?"

"Well, I thought we might excuse ourselves and have dinner at a nice restaurant." John's eyes widened slightly in anticipation of Ali's reply.

"Sounds good to me. The snack foods have filled me a little, but a chicken salad or something light sounds great."

"Cane Garden Country Club has a great chicken salad and it's not far from here. Sound okay?"

Ali gently laid her hand on John's forearm. "That sounds perfect."

John glanced down at Ali's hand and then back to her eyes. He seemed frozen in time by the modest gesture. *This guy's nuts over me,* she thought.

"Cane it is," he said briskly. "Let's go say our good-byes, shall we?" He placed his hand ever so gently on the small of Ali's back, nudging her toward the guests.

* * *

"You're right, John, the chicken salad was delicious. Cane really has good food." She placed her fork on the table and leaned back in her chair.

John was still working on the last vestiges of his French Dip sandwich. Between chews, he said, "Yes, yes, they do."

With John being somewhat preoccupied with finishing his meal, Ali had a few minutes to look him over. Always a little on edge when she was around him, she had never really taken a good hard look at this man with whom she had become involved. Watching him dip his last chunk of sandwich in the small cup of au jus, she liked what she saw. John's thinning black hair was peppered with strands of gray and dangled gently across his broad forehead. It accentuated his soft blue eyes, which were bordered by full black eyebrows. His nose was slightly aquiline, giving a feminine touch to his otherwise chiseled jaw line. His lips were thin, yet attractive. This was a handsome, yet macho, man who would fit comfortably into any football locker room or a Hollywood movie set for that matter. His handsome persona had Ali buzzing inside. Always careful and always in control, this was to some degree, new territory for her. Her eyelids fluttered as John finished his last bite, smiled and dabbed his mouth with his napkin.

"That French Dip was great," he said, dropping his napkin. He paused, pleasantly surprised by the intimate look he was getting from Ali. Always the womanizer, he saw this as a sign that she was possibly starting to succumb to his charm. A broad smile broke out on his face. "You look exceptionally lovely this evening," he said softly.

"Why, thank you, John. What a nice thing to say." She smiled warmly.

John glanced at his watch, "Hmm...it's almost nine, if you will excuse me, I'm going to duck into the men's room and then we can get going."

Ali nodded. *Going where?* she wondered.

Scooting his chair back, he walked briskly toward the restroom, giving Ali even more time to reflect.

Since her breakup with Lex, Ali had dated a few guys she had known in high school, but they did little to stimulate her intellectually. In John, she had found a much different kind of man, well-educated and very successful. She also found him more aggressive and cunning than the local guys. Raised in a strong Christian family, Ali was no pushover and would not compromise herself for any man—rich or poor. She was definitely in new territory with this banker from Tampa and would have to be on her toes.

A few minutes later, John returned and scooted up

to the table. "Shall we retire to my place for a cocktail or two and possibly a dip in the pool?"

"Oh, thank you, John, but I didn't bring my suit."

His right eye narrowed. "I have an eight foot wall around my pool. A suit really isn't necessary, if you get my drift." He reached over and laid his hands on hers.

A warm flush of embarrassment spread up Ali's face. What he was saying was inappropriate, but in some way, it excited her. She had not been with a man since her divorce from Lex three years ago. She began to visualize what John was suggesting. She was tall and shapely and well aware that it would excite any man to see her in the nude. The thought of running around naked with this handsome man by a beautiful pool was titillating, but she had to get control of herself. She couldn't let her foolish fantasies get out of control. She took a long breath, sat up erect, tilted her head submissively to the side, and then ever so delicately, slid her hand out from under his and replied, "I appreciate the invite, John, but I really need to get home. I have an early work day tomorrow and I'm exhausted. I hope you understand."

Dumbfounded, John jerked his hand back and sat up straight in his chair. He didn't reply immediately. His head moved back and forth as if bewildered once again by this unpredictable beauty sitting in front of him. After what seemed an eternity to Ali, he grimaced slightly and replied, "Whatever you say, Ali, whatever you say." He forced a weak smile, stood up next to the table and said, "I'll go find the waitress and get our check and then we can go."

"That would be wonderful, John, thank you."

John hurried off to summon the waitress.

That was close. Ali thought. She hoped she hadn't offended John, but she was relieved she had not gone to his place. The problem she had with John was that she found him disturbingly attractive, even if he was arrogant and overly aggressive. She had fantasized more than once about sleeping with him. After tonight, she felt that her fantasies would only increase in frequency and intensity. She felt vulnerable and conflicted. "How do I get myself in these situations?" she murmured.

Chapter 18

Ned grabbed the towel dangling on the side of his golf bag and dried his sweaty hands. "Man, its hot today," he groused. "I'll be glad when winter gets here and things cool down a little. It must be 95 today."

"It's 92 to be exact, Ned, and it's September, it's always hot in September," one of his golfing buddies replied.

"I know, I know. It's just seems hotter than usual today, that's all."

Ned slid a nine iron out of his bag and walked over to the little white sphere lying in the short rough next to the fairway. A good drive had put him in a prime position for his next shot—a short approach to the last hole. He had a pretty good round going and was hoping to hit this one close to the pin and finish with a birdie. He took his stance, made a couple of quick practice swings, addressed the ball, and then slowly lifted the club back. He swung down at the ball. The Titleist ball exploded off the club face and went soaring high in the air toward the green. Ned watched with great anticipation as it flew through the air and then bounced a couple of times on the fairway, ending up ten yards short of the green.

"What did you hit there?" one of his golfing buddies shouted from across the fairway.

"Nine."

"You never hit enough club, Ned. You should have hit a seven or eight."

"I didn't hit it well, a nine was plenty."

"Yea, yea, that's what you always say."

Ned pushed his backside toward his buddy and jabbed his finger toward it with great gusto. "Kiss this, Wilcox," he bellowed.

Ned's eyes went wide, the other guys in the group suddenly erupted in laughter. Surprised and embarrassed at his outburst, Ned hurried back to his cart, jumped in and sped toward his ball with his cart mate Ben hanging on for dear life.

"That was funny, Ned. Not like you, but funny," Ben shouted.

"Jack's always riding my butt, I just wanted to give him a little of his own medicine." Ned eased off the gas and slowed to a normal speed.

Ben smiled, "Hey, not to change the subject, but I got a question for you, Ned."

"Sure."

"Do you know a John Cullen? I believe he lives in Bridgeport."

"Yea, he lives right near me. I've talked to him a few times, but I don't know him personally." Looking around, Ned eased off the gas again. "Where's your ball, Ben?"

"I'm left, and short as usual."

Ned swerved left and headed toward Ben's ball. "Why do you ask about Cullen?"

"Oh, he's in a group I play with on Monday. He just joined our group a few months ago."

"And?" Ned asked impatiently, anxious to know why Ben had brought up John Cullen.

Ben chuckled, "Well...uh, the guy's about as old as I am and he showed up at our annual golf cookout with this knockdown, drag out, beautiful young gal. She must have been half his age."

"Tall, with dark brown hair and blue eyes?"

"Yes, yes, that's her. How did you know?"

Ned pulled up next to Ben's ball and stopped. "Her name is Ali Brenneman. She was a friend of my daughter's when they were growing up. I saw her the other day at the drugstore where she works and she told me that she was dating John Cullen. And you're right, she is quite a bit younger than him. She's in her mid-thirties and I would guess Cullen to be in his mid-fifties."

"I guess she found her sugar daddy."

Ned turned toward his friend and held a friendly stare. "Not so fast, Ben. Ali is really a nice young lady, I don't think she would ever go out with someone just for their money."

"Uh...huh, and I'm Richard Gere," Ben replied.

Ned smiled, "I've known this girl all her life, and believe me, she's no pushover. I think our Mr. Cullen will find that out sooner or later, if he hasn't already."

"If you say so, Ned."

"I do."

"Well then, there's something else I wanted to ask you."

"Yes?"

"We were over at Pennecamp and a guy in a red Firebird drove by a couple of times. He seemed to be checking us out."

"Do you know if Ali noticed the car or not?" Ned asked.

"Funny you should ask that, Ned, I think she did. My wife and I were making small talk with her and when the car drove by, her expression changed almost immediately. She excused herself, went inside and called somebody. I think something about that car bothered her."

"I'll bet it did."

"Oh yeah?"

"Yeah, her ex-husband drives a red Firebird."

"Oh boy, not good."

"No its not, but we shouldn't jump to conclusions,

it could have been someone else, there's more than one Firebird around here, ya know." Ned was actually stunned by the revelations coming from his friend, but he didn't want Ben to sense how concerned he was about Lex.

"Yea, it was probably just a coincidence."

Ned nodded.

A loud voice suddenly shot across the course at the two preoccupied golfers, "Is this a love fest or a golf game? Hit the damn ball, Ben! We're holding up the whole course!"

Ben grinned, "I guess I'd better hit." Jumping out of the cart, he yanked his wedge out of the bag and hurried to his ball.

* * *

After the round, Ned and the boys were having a beer in the lounge at the Evans Prairie Country Club. About ten minutes into their normal routine of general small talk, Ned took a sip of his Bud Light and stood up. "Hey guys, excuse me for a minute, I need to make a quick phone call.

"Take your time, buddy, we have more fun when you're not here anyway." His foursome all laughed heartily at that one.

Ned shook his head, smiled and ducked out to the clubhouse porch. It was almost five o'clock and he was anxious to try and get ahold of Ali. He dialed her up and waited. It rang twice and then Ali picked up.

"Hello."

"Oh...uh hi, Ali, it's Ned Carpenter calling. I hope I'm not calling you at a bad time."

"Why no, Mr. Carpenter, it's fine. I'm working a double shift today and I'm on my dinner break. What's up?"

Ned took a deep breath and exhaled. Even this seasoned veteran of law enforcement felt uneasy about making this call. "First of all, Ali, what I am about to say is completely confidential."

Ali politely interrupted, "Is something wrong, Mr. Carpenter?"

"I'm not sure, but I have a concern and I would like to talk to you about it."

"Is it about Lex?"

There was a hesitation, "Yes. Why do you ask?"

"Because every problem in my life seems to involve Lex."

"I understand, but it may not even be a problem, I just thought we should talk."

Ned could hear Ali sigh, "Okay."

"I know that you and Lex were very much in love before your divorce, and the whole thing must have been extremely difficult for both of you."

"It was the hardest thing I have ever done, but I felt I had to do it."

"Those must have been trying times for you."

"Yes, they were."

"Ali, it seems to me that you have moved on with your life."

"I feel bad for Lex; but yes, otherwise I'm fine."

"Well, I'm not sure Lex has moved on."

"What makes you think that?"

"Well, I saw Lex drive past John's house a couple of times early in the morning. The first time I saw him, I thought he was looking for an address for a pick up or something, but then he did it again. The second trip raised a red flag with me, so I watched him more closely.

"And?"

"Ali, I think we have a problem on our hands, He really slows down when he drives past John's house, like he's scoping it out."

There was a pause on the other end. "It's all kind of adding up."

"What do you mean?"

"Total confidence, Ned, okay?"

"Always."

"I was at a party last night with John Cullen and Lex drove by in his Firebird a couple of times. It really made me angry, so I went in the house and called him right away."

"Good. What did you say to him?"

"I asked him why he was driving by a party I was attending. He said he wasn't driving by some party I was at. He said he was just looking for someone—a friend who owed him money. Then he said I was crazy and making things up. That infuriated me, so I told him to never come around me again when I'm on a date."

"How did he take that?"

"He got mad and told me that he couldn't care less about me and my, excuse the expression, pansy-ass boyfriend."

"He got defensive."

"Yes, amazingly defensive, but I didn't care, I was too angry with him. I told him that I was serious about this and if he continued to follow me around, I would call my attorney and get a restraining order against him."

"Really! What did he say to that?"

"He got quiet for a second and then told me to leave him alone and quit bothering him." Ali was silent for a second and then spoke quietly, almost mumbling, "I'm sick and tired of him trying to control my life. He seems obsessed with me and John. I wish he could find himself a nice girl friend and just leave me alone."

"I'll bet you do." Ned rubbed his chin for a second and then replied, "I'm out at Evans Prairie right now. Let me think about this and call you back later. What time would work for you? I stay up pretty late."

"The store closes at ten, so you can call me after work if you like. I usually get home around ten thirty."

"Okay, Ali, I will call you then."

"Thank you, Mr. Carpenter. I appreciate your concern."

Ned chuckled nervously, "Once a cop, always a cop. Besides, I've known you since you were a little girl and I just want to be sure everything is okay. "

The phone went dead for a second. Then Ali spoke, her voice trembling slightly, "Thank you so much, Mr. Carpenter. Talk to you later."

"Sure thing. Good-bye, Ali."

"Good-bye, Mr. Carpenter."

Chapter 19

Lex flipped on his turn signal and turned right onto highway 48 W. He felt woozy and sedated. The pot he had smoked earlier in the day was still working on him. He held tightly to the steering wheel to keep from weaving over the center line. A few miles later, he signaled for a left turn onto Laflam Road, the last leg of his drive home. While bumping over some nasty potholes, he carefully scanned the high weeds alongside the narrow road looking for his driveway. Suddenly a tilted, gray metal mailbox with the lid dangling open appeared—he was home. He took a quick right and exited onto his heavily rutted dirt driveway. The Firebird rumbled along the bumpy drive for a few hundred feet and then pulled to a stop in a squared off gravel area covered by little patches of weeds. He pushed the driver's side door open and started to get out. Clutching tightly to a little white sack, he lifted his Diet Coke out of the center console and climbed out of the car. Tired and hungry, he was anxious to get inside, relax and have a bite to eat.

"Damn it!" Lex exclaimed as his left arm bumped against the half open screen door. Testy and with his hands full, he glanced at his arm, and then gave the front door a hearty kick. He paused and smiled as the old door swung open. Lex never locked the door, joking to his friends that "nobody would ever try to break into this piece of shit."

When he stepped inside, he was greeted by the sweet, musty smell of pot. The odor permeated the room as he approached his only chair—a large blue cloth recliner. He fell backward into the chair and dropped the sack on a wobbly TV tray. The tray teetered momentarily and then calmed. He set the soft drink on a sturdier wooden end table on the other side of the chair. Snatching the protruding straw from the bag, he ripped the paper off one end and blew into the other end, sending the narrow wrapper flying. He watched the wrapper glide across the room and land next to a pair of dirty boots. He reached into the white sack and pulled out his Big Mac.

Big Mac in hand, Lex settled into the big recliner, grabbed the remote off the TV tray to his left and punched on the TV. Lex liked reality TV and his favorites shows were the Dateline murder mysteries that aired on CBS. He glanced at his Timex dangling loosely on his wrist, it was just after nine o'clock. A Dateline mystery was about to start. He pushed in the CBS number on his remote and waited while the channel tuned in. He was just in time. The title of tonight's episode, "The Perfect Crime" flashed across the screen, followed by images of a beautiful blond girl and a badly burnt SUV. As usual, Lex was riveted to the screen, almost eating his Big Mac subconsciously as he watched the story unfold on the screen.

Following the dramatic introduction, the narrator, Keith Morrison, set the scene for the night's episode. Warning the viewers that due to the graphic nature of some of the scenes, parental guidance was advised. He then proceeded to describe the events that led to a grisly murder in this rural farming community. In this episode, a young doctor who had just moved to town made the mistake of becoming involved with a beautiful girl who was the receptionist at his clinic. Morrison reminds the viewers about how rare murders are in rural America, especially one involving a local doctor.

The girl, who had been married to a blue collar guy, had recently gone through a nasty divorce. By all accounts, her ex was still madly in love with her. The more the ex-husband saw her and the doctor together, the more jealous and angry he became. At one point in the story, he confides to a friend, "If I can't have her, nobody will." Lex stopped eating and stared at the screen. *That's how I feel,* he thought.

As the story progressed, the young construction worker begins researching methods of eliminating the doctor from his life without getting caught. After considering several dastardly alternatives, he decides that the simplest and cleanest way to do away with the doc would be to shoot him in his SUV and then set the auto on fire, thereby destroying the auto and the body inside. In the process, all the evidence would also be destroyed. His research showed that fire was the best way to commit the perfect crime because it totally eliminated all DNA, hair follicles, fingerprints, and other incriminating evidence.

The jealous ex-husband lured the doctor to a remote park near a small lake on the outskirts of town late one evening, under the guise of making amends with him. The naïve young doctor, anxious to smooth things over with the angry ex, shows up with the best of intentions, only to be greeted by a bullet to the head from a 38 revolver. The angry assassin then douses the doctor and his SUV with over ten gallons of gasoline and sets the whole mess on fire, destroying all of the evidence.

After committing what he hoped was the "perfect" murder, the man drove back to his mom's house and climbed into his bedroom through an open window. The TV he was watching when he left was still blaring when he returned—thus his alibi. His mother would later testify at the trial that she was at home and awake the entire evening and that her son had never left his bedroom because she could hear him watching TV.

Engrossed by the story, Lex's eyes narrowed as Morrison tells the viewers about the riveting conclusion to this true-life mystery. The narrator goes on to explain how the construction worker had nearly committed the perfect crime—except for one small detail. When he reached into his pocket to grab the Bic lighter to ignite the fire, the receipt from the purchase of the lighter and the plastic gas cans fell out on the asphalt parking lot. In his haste to exit the scene, he had failed to notice the little receipt lying next to a parking bumper. Unfortunately for the young assassin, the receipt contained a lot of information, including where the cans had been purchased and the date and time of purchase. The police would later review the security tapes at the local Walmart where he purchased the cans. By examining the video, they were able to identify the ex-husband as he went through the checkout lane with gas cans and Bic lighter.

"Son of a bitch!" Lex groans. Disappointed that the young man had been caught, Lex fell back against the chair and flicked off the TV. He glared out the dirty front window for a few seconds and then mumbled, "The dumbass had him gone! He had it in the bag!"

Chapter 20

John slid onto the barstool, leaned up, and observed the bartender bent over and picking something up from behind the bar. "Hey, barkeep, got any beer back there?" John barked.

Fritz stood up, fallen church key in hand, and smiled at his good friend. "Hey, John, Bud Light coming right up." Fritz washed up and quickly dried his hands. He slid open the lid on the freezer compartment, pulled out a frosty mug and stuck it under the tap. John was impressed by the effortless motions of the muscular bartender.

"You're the best," John quipped.

Fritz set the beer on the bar in front of John. "Thanks, ole buddy. And where have you been keeping yourself?" The barkeep continued washing mugs and checking inventory while he chatted with

John.

"Working in Tampa. I've got a job, ya' know." John lifted his beer and took a sip.

"I guess banking is work." Fritz threw John a sly smile.

"Hey, nine to five, buddy, every day."

"Wow, how do you take it?"

John shook his head, "It's tough, but somebody's got to do it."

"How's your love life? Still seeing Ali Brenneman?"

"Yes, kind of."

Fritz glanced at John, begging more information, "Kind of?"

John chuckled nervously, "Well, things go so far with her and then that's it."

Fritz's eyes widened, he let out a big belly laugh, "What did I tell you? You've got to learn to listen to your old buddy Fritz!"

"I know, you were right. So tell me, smart guy, is there anything else I should know?"

"There sure is." Fritz paused and looked toward his friend, "It ain't going to get any better, John, that's for sure. You have to understand one thing about Ali. She's nice and all that, but she doesn't take any shit off anyone." Fritz laughed again.

John took in a long hard drink of beer and replied, "We'll see."

"A leopard doesn't change its spots, John."

"Like I say, we'll see."

"Okay, Romeo, you may be the only stud to ever score with Ali Brenneman."

John smiled broadly, "Hope so."

"Has Lex been bugging you at all?"

"Her ex?"

"Yeah."

John fell back against the barstool and thought for a second, "I don't think so. I've seen a red car, a Firebird, I believe, around a time or two when I'm with her. She kind of zeros in on it for a while, but that's about it. She's never said anything to me about it."

"Interesting."

"Why, do you say that?"

"Red Firebird, that's him! The guy drives a red Firebird and it's the only one I've seen around here.

"Could be a coincidence or something."

Fritz shook his head disgustedly, "And you're a bank president?"

John laughed, "I remember you warned me about him, but I still don't understand why he would be so worried about an old guy like me?"

Fritz roared, "Oh, for about a hundred reasons or so."

"Such as?"

Fritz stopped cleaning for a second and laid his hands on the bar. "Well, let's see, I wonder if it might bother him just a little bit that you're rich, well-connected, and able to give Ali all the things in life that he could never dream of giving her. Hmm...I wonder if that bothers him. Or the fact that you drive a very expensive car, live in a big house, and hang out with people that Lex only comes in contact with when he's fixing their car. You're not an old guy to him, John, you're a major threat. You're someone who could be taking his Ali away from him."

John's smile faded. He looked past the bartender at the outside bar area at Cody's. A few seconds later he turned his attention back to Fritz and replied, "You may have a point, but I'm really not too worried about it. Besides, I was an Army Ranger back in the day, I can take care of myself."

Fritz shook his head and chuckled, "Ali has a way of diminishing clear thinking, but promise me you'll be careful, okay? I kinda like having you around."

"Will do."

Fritz smiled broadly, "Sorry for getting so heavy on you."

"No problem, Fritz. When you live like I do, you run into guys like her ex all the time. They don't bother me much."

Fritz grabbed John's nearly finished draft and quickly refilled it. "On the house, buddy." Fritz slid the draft in front of John.

"Thanks, Fritz, you're a good friend. And don't worry about me. Like I said, it seems like I'm always bumping into to some ex-husband, ex-boyfriend, or someone who is upset with me. That's why I have so much security around my house." John chuckled, "It's not easy keeping all these women happy."

"Poor guy."

John grinned, "It's a tough life."

"I feel for you buddy. Hey, how about Seth Curry and those Warriors? They could set the NBA win record this year."

"I know, I love that kid. He can shoot the eyes out of the basket. And guess what?"

"What?"

I'm going to the game the next time they play Orlando. One of my board member's has a corporate suite at the Amway Center and he invited me to the game."

"Wow! Let me know if you can squeeze me in. That will be one hell of a game."

"I know."

With the warnings about Ali and Lex out of the way, John and Fritz settled into a lengthy session of small talk, centering mostly on sports and women. John was happy that Fritz had changed the subject from Ali's ex. Since his divorce, John's love life had been in high gear with sexual conquests too numerable to count. Problems with guys like her ex were to be expected, particularly when the girl is as pretty and shapely as Ali. He would take Fritz's advice and be cautious, but he really didn't expect any trouble from this guy. He was just a pathetic loser as far as John was concerned.

* * *

About fifteen miles south of The Villages in a beat-up mobile home nestled amidst the scrub grass and swamps of central Florida, Lex Higgins took a long, hard drag off his weed and held it in his lungs ever so long. A few seconds later, hot smoke drifted skyward, filling the room with the pungent smell of burnt grass. Alone, frightened and angry, he coughed out the last remnants of smoke and belched out the words "He's dead meat." Then he closed his eyes and fell fast asleep. His arm dropped to the side of the chair, his hand fell open, and the hot stub of the weed fell to the floor. A small whiff of smoke drifted up toward the ceiling. Another burned spot joined the scores of others that dotted the carpet around his chair.

Chapter 21

Exhausted from a busy evening at work, Ali tossed her car keys on the kitchen table, walked into her tiny bedroom and fell backwards on her double bed, cell phone in hand. She laid there for several minutes staring at the ceiling. Ned Carpenter would be calling soon, so she had a few minutes. Ever since she was a teenager, she had this habit of lying flat on her back in her bed and staring at the ceiling. She called it her "staring time" and she used this time to think about things that were buzzing around in her mind. With all that was going on in her life right now, she really needed a little "staring time."

Her first thoughts were about Lex—he was definitely one of the major problems in her life right now. She thought about his troubling early morning surveillances of John's house in Bridgeport and his maddening drive by at the Pennecamp cocktail party the evening before. Both of these were indeed bothersome events, but not that serious in Ali's eyes. She still found it extremely difficult to believe Lex would ever do anything bad. During all their years together, he had never exhibited any aggressive behavior toward her. In fact, she often wished that he would have shown a little more backbone and stood up to her more. His current behavior was clearly out of character for Lex—an anomaly. She was certain that this obsession with John would soon pass and Lex would move on to a new love interest.

The funny thing about Lex's recent behavior, was that Ali's feelings for John really weren't that strong. He was amazingly handsome and he appeared to have money, but she definitely wasn't madly in love with him. In fact, she felt a little uncomfortable around him. For a girl from Ali's background, John Cullen could be a very intimidating person. And up to this point, there had been very little romance between them.

She glanced at her watch, it was ten twenty-two. She still had eight minutes before Ned's call. She folded her hands together and carefully placed them against the pillow behind her head and thought back to the Friday night when she first met John at Cody's.

After a busy week of working long days and hauling her mom all over central Florida to shop for a new dresser in the evenings, she had gone to Cody's with her good friend Jennifer to have a few drinks and unwind. Any thought of meeting a man was off the table that night. Ali was looking for a relaxing evening of conversation with her good friend and then an early night home so she could catch up on some much needed sleep. But life is often full of surprises and that night was no exception. Shortly after arriving at Cody's and finding a couple of empty seats at the bar, Ali felt a tap on her shoulder.

"Pardon me, but is this seat taken?"

"No, not at all," Ali replied as she turned to take a look at the nattily dressed man with the nice voice.

"Help yourself," she replied. She was captivated by this distinguished looking gentlemen as he slid onto the stool next to her. He looked very nice with his neatly groomed hair, handsome tanned face and a lean and muscular frame. Ali suddenly felt energized and not nearly as tired as she had been only a few minutes earlier. She held her gaze longer than was appropriate and then returned to her conversation with Jen.

It wasn't long before there was another tap on the shoulder. This time it was an offer to buy her a drink, which she politely declined, but he wasn't finished. As the evening progressed, he kept finding reasons to talk to her, including the use of the worn-out and painfully obvious old line, "haven't we met somewhere before?" It wasn't long before John's dogged persistence had finally managed to turn Ali's attention away from her friend Jennifer. With her focus completely on John now, Ali's fatigue began to melt away. She soon found herself joking, laughing and feeling fine.

The girls had an understanding—an "every girl for herself" mentality when it came to meeting a guy in a bar. If an interesting man came into play during the evening, the other girl was on her own. It wasn't long before Jen decided to pare off from the uncomfortable threesome. Citing exhaustion from a long week at work, she said her goodnights to Ali and John and scurried through the crowded bar and out the front door.

Ali would later apologize profusely to Jen for deserting her in favor of John, even though her actions were well within the rules of the game.

The delightful conversation between John and Ali continued for some time that first night with Ali laughing more than she had for a long time. And John made sure that the liquor continued to flow by ordering Ali's wine glass refilled as soon as it was emptied. Not a heavy drinker, Ali began nursing her drinks to avoid becoming too drunk and too defenseless. Engulfed in an intimate haze of pleasant conversation and laughter, the minutes and the hours seemed to just melt away. Closing time passed and the bar emptied with nary a whiff of recognition from the two garrulous courtesans.

"Sorry," the bartender barked, "but the bar is

closed."

"Closing time?" John groused. He slid his arm off the back of Ali's barstool to look at his watch. "Hmmm, he's right, it is after twelve. I guess time flies when you're having fun." He laid his arm around Ali's shoulder and pulled her closer to him, "Your gorgeous, you know that?"

"Oh, thank you," she said as she ever-so-gently pushed John's arm away.

Ali looked around, and to her surprise, the bar was empty. Somewhat embarrassed and anxious to leave, Ali politely thanked the bartender, gathered her belongings and led John out the front door and into the warm Florida evening.

"The warm air feels good," John said.

Ali smiled in agreement.

"My car is down near the hotel." John nodded in that direction. "Where's yours?"

Embarrassed by her old Honda, Ali grinned nervously and nodded toward the main parking lot hoping that John couldn't see her car. "Over there."

"Oh yes, I see it. I'll escort you to your car."

"Oh no, no, that's not necessary.

"I insist, it's very late and even though it's safe in The Villages, I couldn't let you walk to your car alone at this time of night."

Ali smiled, but inside she was dying of embarrassment.

It was quiet on the street. And the parking lot was

almost empty, except for a few isolated vehicles. John and Ali made small talk on the way to her car. Just before arriving there, John gently grabbed her arm. "I know it's getting late, but how about a nightcap at my place? I've just finished a major remodel and would like for you to see it."

Major remodel on a house in Bridgeport, this has to be special, Ali thought. She decided to take him up on his offer. "It's really not all that late. I would love to see your place."

Ali's memory got a little fuzzy at this point. She barely remembered the drive to his house, and she vaguely remembered the tour of his house that ended up in his master suite. Once in his suite, she did remember her friendly host laughing and then passing out dead on the bed. Anxious to flee the scene, she gave him a peck on the cheek and hurried to her car.

A vibration on her hand jolted Ali out of her thoughts about that first meeting with John and back to the present. Having turned the sound off on her cell phone while at work, she had forgotten to turn it back on. She lifted her arm off the bed and glanced at the lighted screen on her phone and recognized the number for Ned Carpenter.

"Hello, Mr. Carpenter, how are you?"

"I'm fine, thank you and yourself?"

"Okay, a little tired, but okay." Ali rolled over and sat on the edge of the bed.

"I'll bet you are tired, you've had a long day. I'll try to keep this as short as possible." There was a pause on his end as if he was thinking about what he was going to say to her. "Ali, I've known you and Lex since you were kids. I know both of your families, so I wouldn't say what I'm about to say without giving this a lot of thought."

"Yes sir, I understand."

She could hear Ned take a deep breath. "I'm sorry to say this because I know you still have some feelings for Lex, but I don't think he is thinking rationally right now."

Ali pressed her hand to her cheek, "Do you think he's angry at John, Mr. Carpenter?"

"Yes, I think he is. I believe he is very jealous of him."

Ali's brow furrowed. "Mr. Carpenter, I feel bad for Lex, but we are divorced now and I'm trying to move on with my life."

"I understand, Ali, it's just that sometimes when someone feels they might lose the one thing in life they really cherish, they strike back. An otherwise normal person, given the right set of circumstances, can lose perspective."

Surprised by the seriousness in Ned's tone, Ali stood and began pacing back and forth. "I know things look bad with Lex right now and I can understand why you feel the way you do, Mr. Carpenter, but I can't believe that Lex will do something bad to John. Through all of our troubles, he has never raised a hand to me, never. He's been jealous of me before, that's for sure, but I know he could never really hurt anyone."

"I'm sure you know Lex better than anyone, Ali, but I was in law enforcement for a long time and certain things can push a person over the edge. I've seen it many times before, and I truly believe that is what I'm seeing now with Lex. I fear that he may be about to do something that he will regret for the rest of his life."

Ali didn't share Ned's assessment of Lex, but she respected Ned and knew that he had her best interest at heart. Speaking kindly, she chose her words carefully, "So exactly what is it you want from me?"

Ali could hear papers shuffling. "Tell me this, Ali, has Lex ever talked to you about the possibility of getting back together someday?"

"Well, sometimes I do get the feeling that he would like to have me back, but I think it's control more than anything with Lex. He wants to control me. What's the old saying, 'You always want something you can't have'?"

"Maybe so, but I think Lex believes the only thing preventing him from having you back is Cullen. Unlike the other men you've dated, I think Cullen scares Lex. He's afraid of his money and power."

"I feel sorry for Lex, but I really don't think his feelings for me run that deep, I really don't."

Ned sighed, "I'm sorry, Ali, but I have to disagree with you. I think the guy cares deeply for you and will do anything to get you back."

Ali laughed nervously, "Oh my, this all sounds so serious. I guess I just can't go there. I just don't see it."

"Okay, Ali, I've said enough tonight, but promise me this."

There was a pause. "Okay, go on."

"Promise me that you will call me immediately if anything unusual at all happens with Lex, anything that seems out of the ordinary."

"Like what happened at the cookout at Pennecamp?"

"Yes, anything like that. Please call me right away, okay?"

"Okay, I will, I promise."

"And I will do the same from this end."

"Okay, but I really don't think you have anything to worry about. Lex would never hurt anyone."

"I hope you're right, Ali, I really do."

"Anyway, thank you for caring, Mr. Carpenter. I do appreciate it."

"You're very welcome. Goodnight, Ali."

"Goodnight, Mr. Carpenter.

Chapter 22

"Wow! I saw your ex in a Mercedes Roadster the other day with her dad or someone," Rudy smiled mischievously.

"It wasn't her dad, smartass, and you know it," Lex retorted.

"Whoa! Sounds like you're still in love!"

"Are you serious? I've got my own life to lead!"

"You gotta a life alright, but you sure as hell don't have no Mercedes," Rudy roared.

"Shut the hell up, Rudy!"

Sensing Lex's growing frustration, Rudy reluctantly backed off. "So why'd you drag me into town?"

Lex had called Rudy that morning at the meth farm and asked him to meet him at Taco Bell across from Publix for lunch. It had been a full month since

Lex had started cooking again and he wanted to go over the numbers with Rudy. "

"I wanted to let you know that we are making money," Lex said smugly.

"I was making money before you came into the picture, Lex."

Lex shook his head, "You asked me to come back, Rudy, remember? You said I made the best shit in town."

Rudy grimaced. "Okay, you're a fuckin' genius, Lex. So how much are we making?"

Lex took a sip of his coke, sat up in his chair and looked directly at Rudy. "Do you want all the details, ounces per day and all that stuff, or do you just want the bottom line?"

"I know what's goin' on in the lab, Lex, I'm not an idiot! I know we're making more shit now, just give me the bottom line."

Lex slipped his hand into his front jean's pocket, pulled out a folded piece of paper and opened it up, carefully examining his scribblings before speaking to Rudy. "Okay, here's the bottom line as simple as I can make it. You were doing approximately ten thousand a month before I showed up, and this month we did just about thirty thousand. When we get our mobile unit up and running next month, we should be bringing in about forty thousand a month. And here's the best part, I think by this time next year we could double that."

"Hmmm. Good numbers, looks like you earned your twenty percent."

Lex laughed out loud, "Nice try, Rudy, the deal was twenty-five per cent if I doubled the business."

Forcing a smile, Rudy grunted, "If you say so." Rudy's smile quickly faded, his mood darkened, he stared down at the floor. Lex wasn't surprised by his reaction, he knew Rudy. For all his bravado, he was just an insecure, poor kid from central Florida. The big numbers Lex had quoted frightened him, they took him out of his comfort zone. People like Rudy grew up thinking that success in life was something that only happened to other people, not to him. His life was one of battling for the table scraps of life and never getting them. He had lived an amazingly derisory life, where daily survival was the mantra for the day, not what college you might attend or what new house or car or you are going to buy. Lex had been a sensation in high school, a star athlete, a very popular student. He knew what it was like to be on top of the hill, to dream about a future filled with hope and anticipation—something Rudy had never experienced in his entire lifetime. The thought of making big money was scary to a guy like Rudy.

"Everything is going to work out, Rudy, don't worry."

Rudy's eyes shot toward Lex as if coming out of a trance, "I'm not worried, man." His bluster belied the distant look in his eyes.

"Good, because we are growing, and we have to be even more careful now."

"I know, we've got some customers from Marion County and they tell us that the fuzz are pretty tough on drugs over there."

"Yes, they are. The sheriff's daughter died of an overdose a couple of months ago and he's been on a rampage ever since."

Rudy slid his chair back and started to leave. "Yeah, I hear he loves to bust meth labs."

Lex nodded.

Rudy grimaced, "It seems like the more money we make, the riskier it gets."

Rudy was worried, and rightfully so, but risk was part of growing the business. Lex tried to reassure him, "We're pretty well covered at the lab, Rudy, with the security cameras and all."

"Thanks to me," Rudy bragged.

Lex nodded. "Guess so."

"No guessing about it. All of that security shit was my idea and you know it."

"Okay."

Rudy was looking for reinforcement from Lex, but he didn't get it. Obviously upset, he bumped his seat back with his behind and stood to leave.

Lex quickly got up and pushed his hand toward Rudy, not wanting him to leave without shaking hands. "Keep up the good work, Rudy, it's starting to pay off."

Rudy glanced down at Lex's outstretched hand and then reluctantly gave him a quick shake. "When do I get paid?" he asked.

"Tomorrow," Lex replied. "I'm going to get the pay envelopes ready for the workers tonight. After paying all the workers and taking our cuts, we will have two thousand left in the safe for supplies." Lex had a 12 by 15 metal lockbox that he kept the money in, he referred to it as the "safe". He kept the safe hidden in the ceiling of his mobile home.

"How much will I get?"

"After I take my cut," Lex paused and pulled the paper out of his pocket again and quickly checked the figures, "Your cut will be fifty-two hundred dollars."

Rudy's eyes narrowed, "What's your cut?"

"Eight thousand," Lex mumbled.

"That's bullshit!"

"That was the deal, Rudy. Besides, you're making a lot more than you did before." Rudy knew that Lex would make more than him, but he wanted to vent a little bit.

"If we keep doing this much business, we may have to redo this deal."

Lex took a quick look around the brightly decorated restaurant to see if anyone was listening. He felt very uncomfortable talking about such things in a public place. "No way, Rudy. A deal is a deal."

Rudy grumbled, "I gotta go."

"I'll be out first thing in the morning to pay everyone. I don't have to be at work until nine."

Rudy gave Lex an unenthusiastic nod of the head and then turned and hustled out of the restaurant. Lex watched as Rudy hopped in his old pickup truck and pulled away. Lex fell back into his chair. He sat quietly and watched the cars whiz past on Highway 466. He felt good. His plan was starting to fall into place. The current cash flow from the sale of meth would allow him to save nearly ten thousand a month. He would cook for another month or so and then turn the business over to Rudy and be on his way, concentrating all his efforts on starting his Jiffy Lube franchises. His roadmap to success was starting to take shape and his excitement was mounting. He had one more obstacle to overcome to truly have things the way he wanted them—he had to figure out what to do about John Cullen. His mood suddenly darkened. A scowl came over his face, "With him around, nothing works," he murmured.

* * *

Lex let off the clutch and eased onto 466 for the short ride back to work. His mind was racing. The high he had felt only a few minutes ago was being replaced by his growing anger and resentment toward John Cullen. Irrational thoughts filled his mind when Cullen came to his mind. He knew it wasn't good, but his feelings seemed out of his control. His hopes and dreams were about to come true, but this rich bastard was standing in his way. Lex downshifted to second gear and turned right. His hands were shaking with anger. He knew he had to do something—and soon.

He turned into the parking lot by the shop and cruised toward his spot in the back. The car jerked to a stop, he slipped it into neutral and put the parking brake on. He looked down at his cell and browsed through his contacts, "It's still there," he mumbled.

Chapter 23

You could cut the tension with a knife in this bar located in East Orange County on the outskirts of Orlando. Two rough looking characters with Hell's Angel's Miami embossed on the back of their black leather jackets had just strolled into the busy establishment. The locals stopped and stared at them as they made their way to the bar, laughing and making small talk along the way. For all their bravado, the two unexpected guests looked much like the comic book characters Mutt and Jeff. The tall one was well over six feet tall. His thin build and broad shoulders belied a more powerful man beneath the leather jacket dangling so loosely on his long, wiry frame. His buddy was short, bald, and had so many tattoos on his shiny head that at first glance, it almost appeared as though he had a thin crop of bluish hair.

For the majority of the evening, the two outsiders got along pretty well with the local guys at The Blue Dog laughing, joking and just having a good ole time. Things started to go south when the tall one asked the beloved owner, Maggie, who was filling in for the day behind the bar, what "an old broad like her was doing in a dump like this." This attempt at levity was dramatically off course for two reasons: first, he insulted Maggie, who was only fifty-two years old, by making a punishing reference to her aging persona; and secondly, he followed that insult up with a nasty comment about the quality of her establishment, which Maggie thought was about the greatest thing on this side of the Mason-Dixon Line. Fortunately, Maggie, a battle-worn veteran of the rough and tumble world of biker guys, chose to laugh it off saying, "I guess I'm just a glutton for punishment," thus diffusing the situation before one of the local guys, some of whom may have heard the comment, decided to defend Maggie's honor.

The situation remained civil in The Blue Dog for quite a while after the insulting slur, but it elevated dramatically again about forty minutes later when the short guy, now fully intoxicated and way past funny, shouted out with great gusto, "T...tell the old bitch that we need more fire water."

This inglorious pronouncement with all its bluster regrettably drew the full attention of a local tough named Tony Canero, seated just a few stools down from the Miami party boys. A fifty-six year old retired factory worker from New York City, Tony had moved to Orlando some five years earlier to escape some testy legal issues back in The Big Apple. At six foot four and two hundred fifty pounds, Tony was a force with which to be reckoned. Rumor had it that in addition to working as a foreman for a chemical company, he had been known to provide some big-time muscle for local mob bosses when needed.

The edgy, but sociable Tony had been observing the two Hells Angels for some time and apparently, up to this point, had been able to shrug off their bad behavior. That was until the short guy's latest shout-out to his gal friend, Maggie Callahan. That insulting slur had gotten Tony's full attention. Enraged, he took one last sip of beer and slammed the thick mug hard against the top of the bar. The room suddenly got stone-quiet, you could hear a pin drop. The two bikers stared in disbelief as the massive Tony dropped off his stool and strolled directly toward them. With his fist doubled and an angry scowl on his face he eased up next to the tall guy.

"You've got five," Tony said to the lanky hooligan.

The shocked biker studied Tony's face as if trying to figure out his next move. "I don't loan money to strangers," he replied.

"I don't want five dollars, dumb-ass! I'm telling you that you've got five minutes to pay up and get the hell outa here." Tony moved closer to the man, their faces were only inches apart.

Beads of perspiration broke out on the gangly thug's forehead. He turned away from Tony and looked at Maggie who was standing motionless behind the bar. After a slight hesitation, he turned back toward Tony. "We didn't mean the lady any disrespect. We didn't know she was the owner."

"It doesn't matter whether she is the owner of not. We don't treat ladies that way around here."

Realizing this situation was getting out of hand, Maggie spoke up, "It's okay, Tony, I don't want no trouble," she pleaded. "We had a shooting here a few weeks ago and the cops are watching this place like a hawk."

Tony glanced at Maggie and smiled, "Don't worry, Maggie, I'm going to take care of this punk with my bare hands."

With Tony temporarily distracted, the tall one slipped his hand into the inside pocket of his leather jacket and pulled out a bone-handled switchblade knife. Tony saw him from the corner of his eye and immediately went into action, knocking the knife from his hand and then punching the devious biker hard to the gut. With the tall one folded over in pain, big Tony grabbed the other guy who was starting to bolt for the door. He spun him around and delivered a crushing blow to the pudgy devil's face sending him flying to the ground next to the knife. Tony looked down and gave the knife a hard kick, it went flying across the room. Leaning over, he grabbed the thick gold chain around the short guy's neck and yanked him up to eye level. Then he threw his arm around the tall guy's neck and started dragging the two dazed combatants toward the front door.

Once outside, Tony dragged the men over near their bikes and shoved them to the ground. "Now, hop on your fuckin' Harleys and ride outa here! If I ever see either of you around here again, I'll knock your damn heads off!"

Several of the patrons who had followed Tony outside began shouting obscenities and spitting at the men as they mounted their bikes and slowly pulled away from The Blue Dog.

With his hands on his hips, Tony stood and watched the battered and humiliated Angels ride away. One of the men turned around for a brief look back. Tony lifted his fist in the air and shook it at the man. Satisfied that he had defended Maggie's honor, he glared at the departing biker a second longer, then turned and headed back to the bar. Nearing the front door, Tony felt a vibration on his thigh. "What the...," he groused as he quickly slipped his cell out of his jean's pocket. He didn't recognize the number.

"Tony!"

"Yeah, who's this?"

"It's me, Lex."

A small grin appeared on Tony's red, sweaty face. "Lex, buddy! How you doin'?"

"Good, Tony, I'm doing good."

"I haven't talked to you since you got out of the slam. What's goin' on?" Tony held the phone to his ear and plopped down on a bench outside the front door. The other men filed past with several exchanging knuckle bumps with Tony.

"Yeah, things are looking up over here. I'm doing good."

"I'm glad to hear it, Lex."

"You doin' okay, Tony?"

Tony grinned, "Couldn't be better, I just had to toss a couple of guys out of Maggie's place; but all and all, I'm doing just great. And you won't believe this, Lex, but some of the guys got sick at the plant where I used to worked. They started a class action lawsuit and we all got a huge settlement from Dow."

"You're kidding!"

"No, I'm dead serious, it was a nice chunk of money. I'm livin' large man, livin' large." Tony hesitated for a second and then continued, "By the way Lex, before I forget, I've never had a chance to thank you for not ratting me out, you know, back in the day." Tony laughed nervously.

"I take care of my friends Tony. You can always count on me."

"You're a hell of a guy, Lex, I mean that."

The phone went quiet. "Lex, you still there."

"Yeah, I'm here. Are you somewhere where you can talk?"

"Yes, I'm out front by myself. Why, what's so important that I have to be by myself?"

Lex hesitated and then spoke so quietly Tony could barely hear him. "You told me once that you roughed up some guys for the mob or something."

"Yeah...yeah, I roughed up a few guys, but that was a long time ago."

"Well, that's what I called about my friend. I'm having a little problem over here and I could use your help."

"Problem? I thought you said you were doin' good."

"Well, I am, it's...uh it's about Ali."

"What about Ali?"

"We're divorced now."

"You are? Sorry to hear that. She's a doll—one of my favorite people."

"It's been over three years, Tony, and I still miss her."

"I'll bet, but what does all this have to do with me?" Tony stood and began pacing back and forth. He had a gut feeling about what was about to come down, and it was making him a little nervous.

"She's gotten involved with this banker, some rich guy from Tampa."

Tony stopped pacing and stared at the passing traffic, "Well, she's a free woman, I guess she can get involved with whoever she wants."

Lex's voice took a serious tone, "You don't

understand, Tony, I still love her and I want her back. I'm starting to make some money now and I will soon be purchasing my first Jiffy Lube franchise. After that, I plan on owning several Jiffy Lubes. I know she'll come back to me if she can see a future with me."

Tony didn't like what he was hearing. He knew Ali. Not only was she gorgeous, she was a real classy gal. He remembered the first time he met her when he and Lex were in the meth business together. Tony couldn't believe that she had hooked up with a guy like Lex. Their marriage was a serious mismatch. Tony knew what Lex was about to ask him to do and he didn't want any part of it. "Hey buddy, I love ya', you know that, but I don't see what all of this has to do with me."

Lex laughed nervously, "Well...uh this guy could really mess up my plans. He could ruin things between Ali and me."

"Hey man, I'm happily retired in Florida. I've mellowed out, I don't mess with people anymore."

Lex replied irritably, "I saved your ass, Tony. I went to the big house for two miserable years and got fined fifty thousand dollars. I'm still in debt up to my ears."

Agitated and feeling a little guilty, Tony kicked at the loose gravel in the parking lot. Lex was right—he did owe him big time. And even though he regretted ever getting involved with a low-life like Lex, he did take the rap for both of them when he was arrested.

He could have easily implicated Tony, but he didn't.

"Look, Lex, I feel for ya', buddy, I really do, but I should have never gotten involved in the meth business in the first place. I was down and out at the time and needed some cash, but that's all in the past and I'm ashamed for ever having been a part of it. I've righted the ship now and I want to keep it that way."

Lex persisted as if he hadn't heard a word Tony said. "Ali's too good for this guy. I need him out of my life. If you could just rough him up a little, that should do the trick. I'm sure he would scare off pretty easily. Besides, she doesn't mean anything to him, he's just using her."

"You're asking a lot of me, Lex, I just don't think...."

Lex interrupted, "Think about it, Tony, I'll call you back tomorrow at about the same time. Gotta go." He abruptly hung up.

Tony stuffed his phone back into his pocket and sat staring at the ground. Even though he had just wiped up the floor on a couple of Hell's Angels from Miami, Tony was not the same guy he was a few years ago. Getting involved in something like this at this point in his life didn't add up to him. But Tony was also a man who prided himself in always having his friends' back. "Damn!" he grumbled. He shook his head disgustedly, turned and made his way back into The Blue Dog Saloon.

Chapter 24

Ned sat back on his heels, slipped the handkerchief from his back pocket and dabbed the sweat from his brow. It was a warm, muggy fall day in central Florida. He wondered if he had picked the best day to do his annual planting of mums. The heat and the humidity were certainly making it a challenge. With three planters still left to plant, he was hot and tired.

Being alone in his yard for several hours had given Ned a chance to think—mainly about Lex Higgins and his neighbor John Cullen. The situation between Lex and Cullen appeared to be worsening, but when he brought it up to Ali, she downplayed the situation. Ned was a good judge of character and his gut was telling him that Lex Higgins was starting to unravel. With or without Ali's blessing, he felt that he must keep an eye on the situation before it got out of control and Lex did something he would regret.

Ned leaned down and resumed digging in the loose dirt near the front door of his house. It was late afternoon, the hottest part of the day, and he was sweating profusely. He shook the yellow mum from the planter and gently placed it in the ground, carefully pushing the dirt in around the roots of the flower. Lifting the watering can sitting on the ground next to him, he gave the whole area a good dose of water. After setting the can down, he fell back on his heels once again and quickly wiped his brow with the damp handkerchief.

Earlier in the day, Ned was able to plant three or four mums before each break, now he was pausing for a short break after each planting. He looked down at the two remaining planters hoping they might magically jump out of the pallet and into the ground. After several seconds of staring, he was sure that that wasn't going to happen. Starting to reach for the next planter, his attention was suddenly drawn to the sound of loud mufflers coming down his street. Within seconds, a large black pickup truck with over-sized rear wheels came rolling into Bridgeport.

Who in the world could that be? No one around here drives a pickup like that, he thought.

Ned was impressed with the size and sound of the truck as it drove into the neighborhood. The guy behind the wheel was a big, menacing looking sort with wrap-around sunglasses. He seemed to be looking intently at John Cullen's house. *This guy's no neighbor,* Ned thought. *Does he have something to do with Lex and Ali?*

Ned checked out his tags. The plates were registered in Orange County, Florida, the Orlando area. The driver drove ever so slowly to the end of the street, did a quick U-turn and came back the same direction. Once again, the driver gave the Cullen house a good going-over, even goose-necking a little in an effort to see the backyard. Ned sat motionless hoping the man wouldn't see him. The driver cruised slowly past Ned's house, never glancing in his direction. Relieved, Ned watched as he drove on out of the neighborhood, revving the engine just before blending into the traffic on Buena Vista Boulevard.

Ned's sense of alarm went into major overdrive. This guy was up to something and he definitely wasn't a neighbor or anyone Ned had ever seen before. He was not a Villager and he didn't appear to be visiting anyone. The only thing that seemed to interest him was John Cullen's house. To Ned's way of thinking this man was more than likely involved with Lex Higgins.

Then he paused for a second and thought back to his discussion with Ali and her admonition that Lex was not capable of anything bad. All of a sudden a little doubt crept into Ned's thoughts. The guy in the truck had probably heard about The Villages and was just looking around. Certainly nothing wrong with that. And John Cullen had one of the best landscaped yards in Bridgeport--no wonder it caught the driver's eye. Ned took a deep breath and shook his head. He leaned forward, set the next planter in the hole and pushed the dirt tight around it. *Probably nothing,* he thought.

Chapter 25

It had been a wonderful evening starting with a lengthy dinner at the Havana Country Club, followed by a visit to the beautiful Sharon Auditorium for the latest rendition of the classic musical, "Fiddler on the Roof". Now they were back at John's place preparing to take a late evening dip in his kidney shaped pool. When asking Ali out for the evening, John had mentioned to her that they might end up in the pool. Seeing no harm in it, Ali had agreed. She assumed there would be several couples at his house, as was the usual when she was with John. To her surprise, when he picked her up for the evening and walked her to the car, the backseat was empty. When she inquired as to where everybody was, John simply smiled and said everyone had other commitments. She considered backing out of the pool part of the evening, but that would have been awkward, so she decided to soldier on.

The white zinfandel had flowed freely all evening for Ali. It began with a glass in the vestibule before the play and then one at intermission. Followed by at least two more glasses after arriving at John's place. Normally, Ali was a fairly disciplined person, but the wine was causing her inhibitions to weaken. As the evening progressed, Ali began feeling more and more playful on this warm Florida night. Maybe it was the wine and maybe it was because John had looked so handsome when he picked her up earlier in his tailor-made suit, blue button down dress shirt and burgundy tie. Or maybe it was because he smelled of Obsession, her favorite cologne with its intoxicating vanilla-musk scent. Or, even more likely, it was because Ali hadn't been with a man since her divorce from Lex three years ago. Whatever the reason, she felt herself moving into new and uncharted territory with John. It made her more than a little nervous. On the other hand she kind of liked it.

After changing into her bikini in a spare bedroom, Ali made her way to the pool. Feeling seductive and very much aware that John, already in the pool, was watching her every move, she slowly slipped out of her robe at the edge of the pool. She hoped that John was turned on by her skimpy bikini. Chest protruding, she lifted her recently filled glass of wine off of a poolside table, walked to the nearby ladder and eased herself into the pool.

Once she was in the pool, John wasted no time in swimming over to her. She felt his hands slide ever so gently around her waist. He smiled and began pulling her out to deeper water. Feeling aroused, she playfully wiggled out of his grip and swam toward the other side of the dimly lit pool. John laughed out loud and swam after her. With romantic music playing in the background, he moved near to her. Soon, their faces were only inches apart. She felt his hands on her hips, he pulled her closer and planted a warm kiss on her forehead. Ali didn't resist.

"Did you enjoy the play?" he asked softly.

Ali looked into those beautiful blue eyes and perfectly sculpted tanned face and replied, "Sure did, handsome." Ali knew that the "handsome" remark would open the door even wider for him, but she didn't care. She was tired of being the good girl all the time. She was ready to let herself go and experience all the forbidden things she had always been so deprived of.

Encouraged, John carefully lifted the wine glass from Ali's left hand and set it carefully on the edge of the pool. Without speaking, he smiled warmly, looked directly into Ali's eyes, and moved closer. She could feel his warm breath on her face and smell the sweet scent of the wine. With her defenses weakening, she looked longingly into those baby blues. He moved forward for another kiss. She didn't resist, wanting very much to feel his sexy lips next to hers. The kiss was gentle and sensuous. He pulled her closer, their bodies were now merged into one. Her long denied sexual energies were exploding inside of her. She felt his hand slide lightly across her back and carefully untie her bikini top. The straps fell to her sides. The only thing holding her top up was their tight embrace.

The long passionate kiss continued as she ran her fingers through his soft, wavy hair. Then, without warning, John moved back slightly allowing the bikini top to drop off. She looked down at her bare breasts and watched the skimpy top float away. Ali was now face to face with a man and bare-chested for the first time in years. John glanced down at her full, firm breasts and then looked into her eyes. He pulled her close again. She felt the soft hair on his chest brush against her breasts as they began kissing passionately once more. Ali knew this was wrong, so wrong, but she just couldn't help herself. Always the good girl in the group, she didn't want to stop. She felt his hand move down her back and into her bikini, gently caressing her bottom. Then he grabbed the bikini and pulled it down. She kicked her legs free of the tiny bikini bottom and sent it drifting to the top of the pool. She was now in a pool with a handsome man and totally naked.

"I want you, I want you so badly," she moaned. Suddenly, John let out a deep guttural sound, a sharp sickening noise that startled Ali. Shocked out of her amorous mood, she frantically pushed away from him. Terrified, she looked at his face. His eyes were dark and hollow. He suddenly began to drift away from her. She watched in horror as the water in the pool turned red around her. John made an awful, revolting sound that seemed to come from deep inside his body and then everything went black—a cold, forbidding black. Completely horrified, Ali screamed. A loud, terrifying scream!

Chapter 26

Ali flailed wildly at the noisy alarm clock, finally hitting the elusive snooze button. She rolled over, rubbed the sleep from her eyes and looked back at the clock. *Oh my goodness! I'm going to be late for work!* She slid her robe off a nearby chair, slipped it on and headed for the bathroom. "I'm going to need a cold shower after that dream," she mumbled as she pushed through the bathroom door and slipped off her robe. "That was something!"

After the quick shower, she threw on the clothes she had laid out the night before, slapped on some blush and lipstick, pinned her hair back in a bun, and headed out the front door to her car. Still feeling somewhat aroused and confused by her dream, Ali plopped down in the front seat of her Honda and dug furiously through her cluttered purse, finally locating her well buried keys. Wasting no time, she snatched the keys from her purse, stuck the key in the ignition and started up. It was seven forty-five and she was supposed to be at work by eight and it was approximately a thirteen minute drive to work. Barring any unforeseen delays she would make it, but it was going to be close, very close.

Suddenly, her phone blared from inside her purse. She reached in, pulled it out and swiped in on. "Hi, Mom, sorry I didn't answer your call earlier, I was in the shower."

Ali took a deep breath, "I know, Mom, I should have called you back, but I was running late and I didn't have time. And yes, everything is fine and I'm on my way to work right now."

Ali listened patiently and replied. "I'm sorry you were worried, Mom, but I'm okay. You don't have to worry anymore. I will call you tonight. Good-by, Mom." Ali slipped her phone back into her purse

After the annoying call from her mom, Ali's thoughts went back to that dreadful dream. She really wanted to talk to somebody about it. It was so vivid and realistic. It wasn't like her to confide in someone about something so personal, but she had to talk to someone, but who? She hit the gas and pulled out onto Highway 27.

"Jennifer!" she suddenly exclaimed, "I'll call Jennifer." She had bumped into Jen at the grocery store the night before and she told Ali that she had the day off today. Jen was Ali's best friend and she was an early riser, never sleeping past six thirty in the morning. Ali slid her phone out of her purse again and punched up Jennifer.

"Morning, Ali. It's so early, this must be a butt call."

"No it isn't smarty, I just needed to talk to someone and I know you are an early riser."

"That's correct, sweetie, I've been up for over an hour."

"Good."

"Well, go on. This must be important because you are calling me on your way to work, I can hear the car radio."

Ali leaned up and turned off the radio. "Well, it is kind of important, I guess."

"Uh-huh. Well, go ahead, girl, let it fly."

Ali paused to collect her thoughts. "Well...uh, I had this sensuous and scary dream last night. It was so realistic, it really has me reeling."

"Okay, okay, go on."

Ali tapped the steering wheel nervously, embarrassed to tell her good friend all the titillating details of her recent dream. "Well, you know me, Jen, Little Miss Priss and all."

Jennifer chuckled into the phone, "I like Little Miss Goody-Two-Shoes better."

"Okay, smarty, I guess you've never had a naughty dream."

Jennifer laughed this time, "Oh, just about every night! Then again, I'm not Miss Goody-Two-Shoes."

"The dream concerns me because it was about me and John."

"Oh, please, don't let that bother you, Ali, I've had dreams about him myself."

Ali's eyes flew wide, "You have?"

"No, dummy, just kidding. And please hurry up, you're going to get to work soon and I will never hear the torrid details of this naughty, scary little dream my perfect friend had."

Ali flipped on her turn signal and turned off 441 onto 466. "Well, in my dream we had dinner at Havana and then went to a play at The Sharon. After the play, we went back to John's house and took a dip in his pool. We were both a little drunk."

"Wow! Did ya get naked?"

"Jen!"

"Well did you?"

"Well...uh yes, kind of."

"Tell me girl, how do you get "kind of" naked?"

Ali face flushed bright red. Just telling her friend about the dream embarrassed her to death. "Okay, I was totally naked." Ali was almost whispering now.

"Wow! Wow! I love it! Did anything happen?"

"I don't know. I'm not sure."

"Okay, let me get this straight. You ended the evening in John's pool. Both of you were drunk and you got naked, and you're not sure if anything happened?" Jennifer laughed hysterically.

"It was only a dream, Jen, give me a break!" Ali replied irritably.

Still laughing, Jennifer gradually calmed down. "I'm sorry, Ali, I know why you're worried, but I think it's normal to have dreams like this after you've been dating someone as hot as John—perfectly normal."

"Well, I don't think it's normal and I don't like it."

"Okay, then," Jen paused as if thinking and then continued, "Listen to me, Ali, I think I have a plan that will work for you."

"You do? What is it?"

"I know you are concerned that you might be getting too close with John, and even though this was just a dream, you're concerned that the same thing could happen it real life. Am I correct?"

Ali could see the CVS sign ahead. "Pretty much."

"Well, don't you worry your sweet little head anymore. Here's the plan."

"Okay, go ahead."

"The first time you get in a compromising situation with John, and you're all hot and bothered and worried about your reputation and everything, just call me and I will hurry over to wherever you are and take your place. It would probably be in a dark bedroom or something and he will never know the difference."

Ali had to laugh at her friend's suggestion. "You're terrible, Jen, absolutely terrible."

"I know, but I'm willing."

"I know you are, but hold on, I haven't told you about the scary part of my dream.

"Oh yes, the scary part, please go ahead, I can't wait."

Ali drove past the drive-thru toward the front of the store. "At the very end of the dream, when we are both, you know..."

"Naked?"

"Yes, right at that point John made this awful sound like he was hurt or something. It was a dark, eerie, sickening sound. Frightened, I pushed away from him and then watched in horror as red spread throughout the pool. Then everything went black, dead black."

"Hey, girl, you're getting a little too heavy for me. I'm good at the sex part, but this blood in the pool stuff is outa my league, better talk to your shrink about that one."

Hey, I gotta go, I'm at work."

"Okay, love you, hon, and call me anytime. I loved that dream—most of it at least."

"Love you too, and thanks for listening, I think."

Ali could hear Jennifer laughing as she turned off the phone and started into her parking spot at work. All of a sudden, her phone rang again. She looked at the screen, it was Ned Carpenter, so she answered it. "Hello Ned, I'm running late and I literally only have a minute."

"Okay, it's about Lex. Can we meet at Dunkin Donuts after you get off work? There's something we need to discuss."

"Yeah, sure, that will work. See you about four thirty at Dunkin Donuts." Ali had so many questions for him, but she had no time to ask them now. Her questions would have to wait.

"Okay, see you then. Good-bye."

Bye, Mr. Carpenter, see you later.

Ali's eyes clouded over as she stepped out of her car and hurried into CVS. *Everything is so heavy. All I want is someone to love and someone to love me. That's all!*

Chapter 27

John carefully lined up the last putt on the ninth green at Cane Garden Country Club. It was a nasty fifteen foot side hill putt on a very fast green. There was a lot riding on this putt. His buddy, Al Jenkins, sauntered up next to him and whispered, "No pressure, buddy, but the whole day rests on this putt. You hit it, we win twenty bucks. You miss it and we win zip, absolutely nothing. Now stay loose and give it your best shot."

John shook his head, "Will do." John knew what was riding on the putt, but Al mentioning it only added to his self-imposed pressure. He took his stance, took one last look at the hole, brought his putter back slowly and stroked through the ball. The small white sphere rolled ever so directly toward the hole. It was right on track. John raised his putter in a victory salute and hurried toward the hole to retrieve it from the bottom of the cup, but at the last second the ball broke sharply to his right and lipped out. John dropped his putter and fell to his knees in dismay. The other team began prancing around the green and laughing.

"Damn!" John exclaimed. "I can't believe it didn't go in."

Al walked over and laid his hand on John's shoulder, "Nice try, Johnny, I thought it was in."

"Thanks, Al." Al helped John to his feet and the two men walked slowly off the green toward John's cart.

"Don't worry, my friend, at least we broke even and you're still a millionaire," Al laughed. "Let's go have a pitcher of Bud and bury our sorrows. What do you say?"

"Sounds good, Al, we still have fifteen minutes until happy hour is over."

The two men and their playing partners all shook hands, as was customary after a round, win or lose. Then they hurried to their carts, hopped aboard, and headed towards the veranda at Cane Garden Country Club hoping to sneak in a pitcher or two before the end of happy hour.

* * *

The golfers hustled to the veranda and quickly

huddled around a small table. The waitress hurried over and took their order for a pitcher of Bud Light. A short time later, she returned with a cold pitcher and four glasses just before the happy hour came to an end. John lifted the pitcher and carefully filled each of the men's glasses.

Al took a sip. "This is such an amazing view of the golf course from here with the sun setting behind the palm trees."

"Sure is, I love the view here at Cane," Tom Morris replied before glancing over at John. "What brings you to The Villages on a Thursday, John? You are usually a weekend guy."

"I was getting a little tired of the grind. Thought I'd take a few days off," John replied.

"Tired of the grind, my foot! You've got a condition!" Al laughed.

"Condition?" John queried.

"Yes, I think you've got a bad case of Aliosis!"

The other men, all familiar with John's relationship with Ali Brenneman, laughed out loud at Al's light-hearted ribbing.

A red-faced John smiled at his jocular friend. "Well, I...um might see her while I'm here. That's a possibility."

Al looked at John, left brow hoisted. "What are you doing tonight?"

All three men's eyes were suddenly glued on John.

"None of your business," John replied sheepishly.

The men roared.

Feeling the ribbing had gone far enough, Al decided to cut his buddy a little slack. "We understand, John. She is a beautiful girl. Actually, we're just jealous." He gave his friend a big thumbs up.

"She's a looker alright, that's for sure," Tom added.

"Well thank-you, guys. And speaking of Ali, it's almost six, I have to pick her up at seven at Lake Harris. I hate to rush off, but I best be going."

"Lake Harris, you say. Yeah, you'd better get hustling," Al said.

"I'll see all of you Saturday morning at Hacienda at eight thirty, right?"

"That's right," Al replied.

John quickly gulped down the remnants of his beer, gave each of his golfing buddies a high five, dropped a twenty on the table and hustled to his golf cart parked in the side lot at Cane. Al had switched John's bag back over to his cart before they had a beer, so John was free to go. He hopped aboard the cart and headed for Lakewood Dr. A short time later he flipped on the left turn signal and darted onto Bailey Trail and raced for home.

The cool fall breeze felt good against his sunburned face as he sped along the narrow cart trail. Several autos whizzed past him on the street. John could literally smell their exhaust. A short time later, he merged in with the regular traffic and made a left turn onto the Buena Vista Recreational Trail. He cruised past the Lake Miona Recreation Center, ducked into the tunnel under Buena Vista Boulevard and gunned it north on the path toward Bridgeport.

Cruising toward home, John thought back to the friendly ribbing he had just taken from the guys at the golf course. They were just kidding, of course, but to some degree they were right, John did like younger women. His second wife was only a year older than John, but she looked much older than him. He remembered how as the years passed, he became more and more turned off by her appearance. The heavy crow's feet around her eyes, her sagging neck, dull gray hair, thick legs and varicose veins were disgusting to him. He hated to admit it, but her premature aging was probably one of the main reasons he divorced her. He begged incompatibility in divorce court, but in his heart he knew the real reason for the divorce from his otherwise very loving and caring wife—was simply her looks. It bothered him that he was such a surface person, but it didn't bother him enough to change. Life was good for John Cullen and he wanted to keep it that way.

After passing the exit for Lake Sumter Landing, John ducked into the last tunnel on his trip home and made his way to the entrance of Bridgeport at Lake Miona. Immediately upon entering his village, John took a hard right into the mail drop area. He stopped in front of his mail slot and hopped out of the cart. On the way to the box, he dug around in his pocket and pulled out the key. He tugged the door open to the rarely used box and pulled out the contents. On the way back to his cart, he sorted through the junk mail and flyers. Not seeing anything worth reading, he slid into his cart and tossed the mail on the passenger side seat. Before leaving the mail area, he pulled out his cell phone and rang up Ali.

"Hello?"

"Hi, Ali, it's me."

"I know, your name came up on my screen." Ali giggled.

"Oh...uh I suppose it did." John frowned. He knew that he was always a little off his game with Ali. Part of him hated it and part of him loved it.

"Have you finished golfing?"

"Yes, I left the course a little while ago."

"How'd ya hit 'em?"

"Not bad. I missed a putt on the last hole that cost us twenty bucks, but otherwise I played pretty well. Thank you for asking."

"Are you still picking me up at seven?"

"Oh yes, I just called to tell you that there has been a little change in our plans, if you don't mind."

Ali hesitated briefly, "Oh, no problem, no problem at all."

John slipped the cart into reverse and prepared to back up. "Well, instead of dinner and a movie, I thought we might take in a nice dinner at Havana and then go to a play at The Sharon."

"What! Are you kidding me?"

Chapter 28

Once again, Ned was somewhat conflicted about this hastily arranged meeting with Ali, but he knew if he didn't keep her in the loop and something happened to John, he would never be able forgive himself. Ned took a sip of coffee and glanced down at his watch, it was a little after five. Ali had texted him a few minutes ago explaining she would be a little late. Her replacement at the cash register was running behind. A few minutes later, a shadow passed through the restaurant, Ned looked outside as the old green Honda pulled into a parking spot near the front door. Ali jumped out the driver's side and headed inside. She looked around and quickly spotted Ned. She tossed him a warm smile and walked over next to him.

"I'm so sorry I'm late, Mr. Carpenter, but Lisa's

husband was late getting home from work and they have two little children."

"Don't think a thing about it, Ali, I've been enjoying my coffee and Dunkin Donuts is my favorite." He lifted the cup towards her and grinned.

Ali carefully laid her handbag on the counter and sat down on the stool next to Ned. "It's got to be tough when you have small children. I guess I'm fortunate that I don't have that to worry about!"

Ned's brow lifted, "Something tells me that's a problem you wish you had."

Ali's eyes darted toward Ned, as if startled by the insightful comment. She smiled and looked away. "I guess so, maybe someday." she replied quietly.

Ned chuckled, "Well, I didn't ask you here to talk about raising a family."

Ali mood changed. It was obvious she was anxious to know why Ned had asked her to meet with him. "I'm assuming this has something to do with Lex," she queried. The waitress approached and pushed a cup of coffee in front of Ali.

"On me," Ned said. "There's cream and sweeteners right here." He pointed to the display of condiments in front of him.

"Black is fine," she smiled.

Ned took a deep breath and exhaled, "Ali, there's been more suspicious activity in our neighborhood. It might be nothing, but it troubled me and I thought you should know about it."

"Has Lex been driving around the neighborhood again?"

"No, not Lex, but yesterday when I was out planting mums in my yard, a large black truck with Orange County plates came cruising through our neighborhood and the driver paid special attention to John's house. He even made it a point to check out the backyard."

Ali sat up straight, she seemed slightly annoyed. "Well, Mr. Carpenter, there could be a hundred reasons why this guy drove his truck through your neighborhood. He may know someone or have relatives there. Or maybe, like so many people, he just heard about The Villages and was taking a look around. I really don't see what this has got to do with Lex."

"I know you don't see anything here. It's just that...."

Ali shifted toward him and interrupted, "Mr. Carpenter, I appreciate your concern about me, I really do. Our relationship goes back a long way, but this whole thing about Lex and John is starting to get me down, and to be quite frank, I really don't see much there, if you know what I mean."

"I understand completely, Ali, and I thought long and hard before I called you this morning. At first, I have to admit, I was giving this guy the benefit of the doubt and for all the same reasons you just described, but I just couldn't get it off my mind. There was something about the guy in the truck that seemed familiar to me. Then last evening while I was sitting and watching television, it suddenly came to me—I remembered him. I remembered where I had seen him before." Ned paused for a second.

"Go ahead."

"He's not the sort of person who is easily forgotten. He's a big, ruggedly handsome man. I remembered seeing him at the local McDonald's a couple of times several years ago."

"Nothing unusual there, maybe he lives in the area," Ali retorted.

"I am sure he doesn't live around here because I have never seen him since and I have lived here all my life. And anyway, he has Orange County plates."

Ali grew impatient. "Maybe he stops here on his way from Orlando to visit his Aunt Emma or something. I appreciate you looking out for me, Mr. Carpenter, but I've had a long day and I really need to be going."

Ned leaned forward and quickly laid his hand on Ali's forearm. "The two times I saw him, Ali, he was meeting with Lex. Both times it was in the morning and I was having coffee with my friends. It was during the time when Lex was involved with meth. Both times they were sitting in an isolated booth and it was obvious they were having a private conversation. I believe there is a direct connection between Lex and this man from Orlando. That's the only reason I asked to meet with you. We know Lex has been checking out John Cullen's house and we also know Lex is very interested in who you are dating. And now this man is also checking out Cullen's house. Ali, I don't want to alarm you, but the information is starting to add up."

Ali's shoulders slumped. She shook her head and tears welled in her eyes. "I see what you're saying, Ned, I really do. I truly loved Lex at one time and I still care for him. I know he ran with some rough characters during that period, but I just won't let myself go there. I can't make myself believe that he would do something awful to John. The Lex I know would never do anything like that." She forced a half smile, got up off the stool, slid her purse off of the counter and started to leave. "I'm sorry, Mr. Carpenter, but I really must be going."

Ned slipped a five dollar bill from his money clip and dropped it on the counter. "I'm sorry if I have upset you, Ali, but you said you wanted me to keep you up to date on any new developments and I don't like what I'm seeing—I don't like it at all."

Ali's brow narrowed. She shoved her purse under her arm. "It's always us, isn't it, Mr. Carpenter? It's people like Lex and me that do all the bad stuff. We're the ones that are capable of horrible things, us poor folks! Why, if Lex were the son of one of your fancy golfing buddies, you wouldn't think a thing about what's going on. He wouldn't even be on your radar."

Red ran up Ned's face, "Oh my, no, Ali, you know me better than that. My goodness, you're a wonderful girl! I think of you as my own daughter. I would never think less of you, never in a million years."

Ali's chin fell to her chest and she began sobbing. Ned stepped closer and put his arms around her and held her. "I'm sorry, Ali."

"No, I'm sorry, Mr. Carpenter, I'm just so confused about all this. Please forgive me."

"You're right, Ali, I probably am over-playing this whole thing. Nothing has really happened. It's all just supposition at this point." He stepped back with his hands still on Ali's shoulders and looked directly in her eyes. "In the future, I won't bore you with all my Sherlock Holmes theories, I'll just keep it to myself. This isn't your problem anyway. You have your own life to lead. I'm so, so, sorry that I upset you, it won't happen again."

Ali leaned over and kissed him on the cheek. "Thanks for caring so much. You're a wonderful man and I'm sorry for my little outburst, but I really do need to be going." She smiled warmly and turned and hurried from the busy cafe.

Chapter 29

"Did you say dinner at Havana and then a play at The Sharon?" Ali's blood ran cold as thoughts of her recent dream raced through her mind.

"Yes, yes, I did. If that's okay, you sounded hesitant," John responded.

John was right—Ali was hesitant. Taking a deep breath, she tried to compose herself. "Oh no, not at all, that sounds great, John. What will we see?"

A traveling theater group from Tampa will be performing an old favorite, *Fiddler on the Roof*. I saw this group a couple of times in Tampa and they are very good."

The room suddenly went fuzzy. Can this really be happening? It was only two days ago that she had that hideous dream and now John is basically proposing the same evening to her. She felt weak in the knees and panicky. The dream and John's suggestion brought back the painful memories of her grandfather's death. When she was eight years old, she dreamt that her beloved grandfather died of a heart attack. The next day, much to her horror, he actually did die of a massive heart attack. The similarity of the two dreams was surreal. Memories of that terrible dream haunted her to this day. Could it be that her recent dream about her evening with John was another premonition of things to come? Could Ned be right? Is something awful going to happen to John tonight?

"Ali, Ali, are you still there?"

"Uh...yes, I sure am, I just got distracted for a minute. That sounds good, John. Sounds like fun. I'll...uh be ready at seven."

"Seven it is! How about we take a moonlight dip in my pool after the play?"

A bolt of fear shot up Ali's spine. "A dip?"

"Yes, a dip in the pool. Why? Are you okay?"

"Yes...yes, I'm fine. I'd better run now, I've got lots to do." Ali, anxious to hang up, tapped her phone off and fell back in the chair, moving her head rapidly from side to side in disbelief. *This is crazy, so crazy!* She hoped that John didn't call her back; she was in no mood to talk. She stared at the screen for a second and nothing happened. "Good," she mumbled.

Phone in hand, she sat frozen in her recliner, shaken by his invitation. Her recent conversations with Ned Carpenter and his warnings about Lex's behavior only served to heighten her dread about this evening. Could this all be part of some ghastly, awful reality that was about to take place? She was breathing hard, her heart was racing. She got up from the chair and began pacing back and forth. She repeated "calm down" to herself over and over again. Wanting very much to talk to someone, she looked at her phone and punched in Jen's number. The call rang and rang and then went to voice mail. Ali hung up, deciding not to leave a message. She remembered that Jen worked until eleven and couldn't answer her phone when she was working anyway. Still feeling somewhat frantic, she began pacing again. She tried to think of other friends to call, but after some thought, she decided against it. Fearing that they wouldn't understand her awful dream and that she would appear foolish.

It was twenty after six and John was going to pick her up at seven. She had to get ready for her date and pronto. Ali hurried to the bathroom and slipped out of her jeans and cotton shirt. Pulling the shower curtain back, she turned on the hot water and waited for the water to get hot. All the while, the dream kept running through her mind. Was it just a coincidence or was it really a premonition of things to come? Part of her was telling her that this dream sequence was ridiculous and absurd, and another part of her was telling her that it was a case of déjà vu and something awful was about to happen. Would someone be hiding in the backyard at John's house when they got home from the play tonight? If so, would this intruder come out of the darkness and do something awful to John? She thought about Ned Carpenter's warnings about Lex and her haunting childhood dream. Starting to break into a cold sweat, she reached over and felt the water again, it was finally getting hot.

She adjusted the hot and cold to the desired temperature, slipped off her panties and bra and stepped into the shower. The hot water had a calming effect; it felt good on her back. She moved slowly from side to side trying to enjoy the shower and relax. Ali knew that her friends and family would not buy into the dream scenario. They were way too practical and realistic. She had to deal with her fears about this dream on her own. If Jen called back, she would apologize and tell her that the call earlier was an accident, a butt call. She had to resolve this on her own without the help of anyone else.

Ali hastily sponged herself, stepped out of the shower and dried off. Slipping on her terrycloth robe, she hurried over to the medicine cabinet mirror and began putting on her makeup. *You don't look like a crazy woman,* she thought as she put on some eye shadow and then dabbed on a thin coat of lipstick. Blessed with a very smooth and creamy complexion, Ali required very little makeup. Next, she blow-dried her hair, curled her bangs, sprayed on an ample supply of Paul Mitchell and took a look. "Not perfect," she groaned, "but it will have to do." She fluffed her hair and then headed for the closet to put on her black leggings and sequined white blouse.

After dressing, she walked over to her chest of drawers, opened the top drawer and pulled out her black bikini. She thought for a moment, and then dropped the tiny suit back into the drawer. She turned around, pushed the dresser door shut with her backside and stared across the room. Ali knew there wasn't any way she would be able to get in that pool tonight. She would have to come up with an excuse not to go to John's house. No bikini tonight. No pool party tonight. She had made her decision.

Ali bent down and slid on a pair of stylish black sandals. After carefully attaching two pearl earrings, a gift from a previous beau, she took one last look in the full-length mirror and smiled. She was ready. Now she could enjoy the evening without worrying herself sick about that stupid dream. Her smile broadened when she heard the gravel crunching out on the driveway. John was here, it was time to leave. She dabbed a splash of Victoria's Secret perfume behind each ear, snatched her purse off the chest and walked briskly to the front door to greet John.

Chapter 30

Returning from his quick trip to The Villages, Tony slowed his big truck into the fast approaching exit. He was now just a few minutes away from the Blue Dog Saloon. After Lex's troublesome call, he had decided to go to The Villages and check things out for himself. Time was when he wouldn't have given Lex's request a second thought. He would have just done it. But Tony was a changed man. Still rough and ready when need be, he had mellowed a lot over the past couple of years.

His visit to The Villages had been an eye opener. With its beautiful boulevards bordered by lush golf courses with nattily dressed golfers stacked up on every tee, the place had charmed the socks off of Tony. It seemed so friendly and active there. He was certain it would be a wonderful place to live. The few people he had talked to were open and upbeat. How could he go into an environment like that and rough somebody up? His quick trip to The Villages had confirmed one thing for Tony—he couldn't do what Lex was asking of him.

A few minutes later, Tony turned off the busy roadway and coasted to a stop in front of the Blue Dog Saloon. As he started to climb out of the truck, his cell phone began to ring—it was Lex. Tony quickly got out of his truck and answered. "Yea, Lex, what's up?"

"Just checking back with you about what we talked about yesterday. What's it going to be, Tony? Are you going to help me out or not?"

Tony paused on his way into the bar and fell against a large post near the front door. "After I talked to you yesterday, I decided to take a trip over to The Villages and look things over for myself, to try and get a lay of the land, if you know what I mean."

"You what?" Lex sounded incredulous.

"I took a little ride over to The Villages."

"You still have that big black truck?" came the quick response.

"Yes, Lex. So what?"

The phone got quiet on the other end. "Let me get this straight. Big Tony Canero, drove his bad boy black truck with flames on the side and loud mufflers over to The Villages to take a look around?"

"Hell, yes, so what?" Tony replied defensively.

"So what? They're used to fancy cars and golf carts. You had to standout like a sore thumb.

Tony coughed up a nervous laugh, "Yeah, I guess I did get a few stares from the folks."

"Where all did you go?"

"I went to a town center, Sumter something. And then I went to the village this guy lived in to take a look around."

"You went to his village?"

"Sure as hell did."

"Did anyone see you?"

"I saw a few people out in their yards."

"Did they see you?"

"Must have, a couple of them waved at me. They were friendly enough, no big deal."

"No big deal!" Lex had that incredulous tone again. "Tony, you just blew your cover. How are you going to go into The Villages and take care of this guy when everybody in the place has already seen you driving around in that big black truck? I can't believe it!"

Tony stood up from the post, crossed his arms on his chest, phone to his ear. "Calm down, Lex, it doesn't matter."

"Doesn't matter, what are you talking about?"

Tony voice began to rise as he spoke, "It doesn't matter, Lex, cause I'm not doing it. I'm not going to go over to that place and hurt some retired guy who hasn't done a thing to me. I'm just not going to do it."

Lex fired right back, "Have you gone soft or something?"

Tony could feel his face get warm. He unfolded his arms and clinched his fist. He was livid. "Listen up, Lex, don't you ever say that to me again or I'll personally come over to Leesburg and kick your ass. Do you understand me?"

There was another pause. "I can't believe this, I've got a lot at stake here. This is about my future. You owe me, Tony!"

Tony took a deep breath to calm himself down and replied, "I understand, Lex, but I just can't do it."

"That's bullshit! You owe me big time! Think about it some more, I will call you later."

"It won't do any..."

Lex interrupted. "Good-bye."

Tony turned his phone off, stared at the passing traffic for a moment, and then mumbled, "son-of-a-bitch" and ducked in the Blue Dog.

* * *

"Spineless bastard!" Lex mumbled. Feeling shaky inside, beads of perspiration bled down into his eyes. He ripped a wad of toilet paper from the nearby dispenser and wiped his eyes. Lex was falling apart. He wasn't eating right, sleeping well or thinking straight. He was consumed by his hatred for John Cullen.

No saint, Lex had always considered himself a pretty good person. But now, with all that was coming down around him, it was bringing out another side of Lex—a very ugly side. Recently, he had found himself fantasizing about killing Cullen. Violent images of him shooting Cullen in the head or blowing up his car with him inside were frequenting his thoughts. And with this recent bad news from Tony, the depth of his anger was almost intolerable.

Drying his eyes one last time with the toilet paper, Lex stood, lifted the toilet seat and dropped the wad of tissue into the bowl. It was Lex's Saturday to work and he had gone to the bathroom at Tire Hut to call Tony. Hiding in a stall during the call, he hadn't noticed if anyone came in the restroom. Due to the damning nature of his conversation with Tony, he wanted to be sure that no one had heard him. He pushed the metal door open slightly and peaked outside. It was empty, there was nobody around. Feeling better, he walked over to the sink and splashed cold water on his hot, sweaty face. With work still to do, he needed to try and get control of himself before he returned to the garage area.

Ripping a couple of paper towels loose, he began to dry his face. While standing in front of the mirror, he caught a glimpse of himself. The image he saw shocked him. His eyes were dark and lifeless, his hair was dull and messy, and his cheeks were pale and sunken. His appearance had changed dramatically in just the past few days. The emotions that were consuming him were taking a tremendous toll on his appearance. To make matters worse, he had turned back to prescription drugs to help calm his emotions. Still shaking, he stuffed his hand into his jean's pocket and pulled out a small plastic prescription bottle. He shook four Percocet tablets into his hand, turned on the water, leaned over and sucked his mouth full of water. He leaned his head back, tossed the tabs in his mouth and gulped them down. Stuffing the plastic bottle back in his jeans, he turned off the water. *That bastard is ruining my life,* he thought. With his hands still shaking, he wrestled a small black comb from his pocket and ran it through his hair. He straightened the collar on his shirt and hiked up his jeans. Looking a little better, he turned and shouldered his way through the door and hurried back to the garage area to finish the last hour of his shift.

Walking through the busy lounge area, Lex recalled a conversation he had earlier in the day. A nervous Rudy had called him to tell him that he had seen patrol cars near the lab on two separate occasions this week. In both cases, he had decided to leave the area and return to Wildwood to avoid being detected by the police. He also told Lex that on his way back to Wildwood that he had called the workers and told them not to show up if they saw any signs of police near the lab.

Lex had listened intently to Rudy. He had great respect for the local cops. When they got you on their radar, they didn't let up. With Lex's past record, getting busted was not an option. This was big news and it needed to be addressed immediately. Lex had asked Rudy to meet him at the McDonald's in The Colony Plaza Shopping Center at seven-thirty tonight to further discuss the situation. Rudy had agreed.

Chapter 31

Lex hurried home after work to get the money out of his safe before he met with Rudy. Feeling somewhat sober when he arrived home, he retrieved the metal box from above the false ceiling and counted out the money. With the recent spike in activity by the local sheriff's department, Lex felt it was time to split the final proceeds with Rudy and get out of the meth business. He wasn't sure how Rudy would react since Rudy was dependent on the money to support his wife and kids. His gut told him that Rudy would probably try and continue to cook even with the increased attention from the police.

After counting the money in the safe and setting aside enough money to make the current payroll and pay Rudy his cut, Lex was left with nearly ten thousand dollars, up a little from the figures he had discussed with Rudy a few days earlier. Lex already had twelve in the bank, so now he had a total of twenty-two thousand. He smiled, *this will be enough to start my first Jiffy Lube.*

The district manager for Jiffy Lube had reassured Lex recently that he could open his first shop in Wildwood with a minimum of twenty thousand. That would be enough to cover initial supplies, franchise fees, and insurance. They would then lease the building and the equipment back to him for an agreed upon monthly fee. The company had already found a building in Wildwood and told him it could be up and running as early as next month. It wouldn't be long before Lex could schedule a grand opening and move on with his life.

Through the haze of prescription drugs and whisky, Lex was starting to feel a little excited. He could invite Ali to his grand opening and show her his brand new business venture. She would be very impressed. Then he would use the opportunity to ask her out and possibly start seeing her again. That is if he didn't have Cullen around trying to mess things up.

Lex started to feel queasy, every time he thought about Cullen, he felt sick inside. Frightened to death that his money and charm were starting to have an effect on Ali. He had often fantasied about Cullen and Ali having sex together. The very thought of that incensed him. She was a virgin when Lex married her.

He was the first and only man to ever make love to Ali and if he had anything to say about it, he would be the last. *If I can't have her, nobody will,* he thought as he quickly stuffed Rudy's cut of the cash into a canvas bag, grabbed his notes, and hurried out the door for his meeting with Rudy.

As Lex exited into the Colony shopping center, his head was throbbing from the pills and booze. Arriving at McDonald's, he glanced around the parking lot looking for Rudy's old beat up pickup. He couldn't see it at first, but as he rounded the drive-thru area, he spotted it. Luckily, there was an open parking spot just a few spaces down from Rudy's truck. Lex parked and hurried inside.

Lex found Rudy sitting just inside the front door and fidgeting with his car keys. He looked nervous. He looked up at Lex and nodded at the seat across from him, "Sit down," he ordered. There were two cups of coffee sitting on the table, a rare show of generosity on Rudy's part.

Lex sat down. "Thanks for the coffee."

"No problem." Rudy gave Lex the once over. "You look like hell."

Lex shook his head, "Thanks," he replied. Wasting no time, he reached in his little bag, pulled out Rudy's cut of the cash and pushed it over in front of him.

"Not here," Rudy barked.

Lex quickly stuffed the cash back in the canvas

bag. "I just wanted you to see what sixty-two hundred in cash looked like."

"Looks alright."

"It's a lot of money."

"It's not as much as you get."

"I guess not, Rudy, but it's a lot more than you ever got for cooking before."

Rudy shrugged, "I had some good days."

Lex leaned back. "I got something to tell you."

Rudy's brow lifted. "What's that?"

"I'm getting out of the business, Rudy. With the cops all over the place, I just can't risk it. If I get busted again, I'll never see the light of day."

Rudy's eyes flew wide. "What the fuck, Lex, you've only been cooking a few months! You can't back out now!"

"You're not thinking Rudy. With me out of the way, you can keep all the money for yourself."

Rudy fell back against his seat, chin on chest. He was quiet for a while as if pondering the situation. Then he sat up and flashed a half grin. "You're right, Lex. I don't need your tired ass anymore and I will make a lot more money on my own. So good riddance."

Lex knew that Rudy was being sarcastic, but he didn't want to push the situation, so he changed the subject. "I think you ought to consider closing the lab temporarily, until the heat eases off."

"I don't need you to tell me what to do, Lex, you're

out of the business, remember? Anyway, I had planned on shutting it down. I'm not stupid, ya know."

"I know."

The two fiery friends decided to meet at the meth house early the next morning and clear out all the equipment and supplies. They would pile everything in their trucks and haul it to an old shed at the back of Rudy's place for safe keeping. Then, after sharing a few more insults, they stood to leave.

Lex spoke up, "Sorry, Rudy, but I just don't want to go back to jail."

A slightly more contrite Rudy shrugged his shoulders, "Who cares?"

"Why don't you let me buy you a drink for old times' sake?"

Rudy hesitated for a second, "Where?"

"How about City Fire in Brownwood?"

"Okay, I like City Fire." There was an uncomfortable silence, and then Rudy continued. "I have to go to the restroom. My car's unlocked. Just throw the money in the front seat and then lock the door. See you at City Fire."

"Okay, see you in a while."

Rudy nodded.

Lex was starting to feel woozy again as he pulled out of the parking lot at McDonald's. He was glad that he and Rudy had agreed to meet at City Fire and he was glad they were dismantling the meth operation in the morning. With the meth operation closed down and all of the evidence removed, he would be home free. Unfortunately for Lex, the other major problem in his life was much more complicated and not so easily solved. The very thought of John Cullen made him anxious.

He's probably out with her tonight, he thought, as he reached over and opened the glove compartment and yanked out a pint of Jim Beam. He stuck the end of the bottle in his mouth, screwed the lid off and took several swigs. Trapped in a twilight zone full of rage and alcohol, his mood began to darken. He exited left off Colony Drive and accelerated onto Morse Boulevard, barely avoiding a collision with a large SUV as he blended into the heavy traffic.

Chapter 32

"Did you enjoy the play?"

"Oh yes, John, very much. I thought the young man who had the lead had a wonderful voice," Ali replied.

"How about your dinner, did you enjoy your filet?"

"Dinner was delicious, I love the restaurant at Havana. My filet was so tender."

Ali held her gaze on John longer than usual. He looked so handsome in his light blue golf shirt and khaki slacks. The long day on the golf course in the hot sun had deepened his tan. She realized she was becoming more and more attracted to John, and not only because of his good looks, but lately he seemed to be mellowing a bit. Not much, but a bit. She was starting to see a side of John she hadn't seen before—a side that made her believe that he was a man she just might be able to get close to. At this point, she still had some doubts, but things seemed to be moving that way.

"You look lovely tonight, Ali."

"Why thank you, John, and you look very handsome." Ali smiled warmly. The exchange of compliments sent her buzzing inside.

John turned right off Odell Circle onto Buena Vista Boulevard and headed north toward Bridgeport at Lake Miona. Ali's amorous feelings suddenly turned to dread when she realized that they would soon be at John's place. She had been pushing it to the back of her mind all evening, but now with time running short, she had to confront the issue. It was time to tell John that she couldn't go to his house tonight for a swim. This was going to be difficult for her to do after such a lovely evening, but she had no choice. Her intuition told her that something bad was going to happen tonight and she needed to change the course of the evening. She took a deep breath, laid her hand gently on John's forearm and spoke, "Uh...John, there's something I need to tell you before we get to your place."

John's eyes widened, his brow lifted as if to say go ahead.

She continued, "What I'm about to say may sound unusual and it may surprise you. Promise me that you won't think I'm crazy, okay?"

"Well, I'm not sure what this is all about, but I can

assure you, Ali, that I could never think of you as crazy."

"Thank you." She folded her hands on her lap and looked out the front windshield, too embarrassed to make direct eye contact. "John, I am not a superstitious person and I don't believe in ESP or anything like that, but I had this incredibly vivid, awful dream recently. It was so realistic that it really frightened me."

"Okay, I've had my share of bad dreams also. Can't ever remember any of them, but I have dreams all the time. Please, go ahead, I'm anxious to hear."

Ali told him in great detail about her dream from a couple of days earlier. She went over all the major details, including the horrible scene at the end with John gasping and blood spreading throughout the pool. She did take a little liberty at a certain part of the dream, greatly diminishing the intensity of the sexual contact between her and John. When she was finished, she glanced out the corner of her eye at John hoping to gage his reaction.

He chuckled, nodded and then reassured her that it was only a dream and not to put too much stock in it. Somewhat annoyed by his condescending tone, she immediately told him about the dream she had when she was a little girl about her grandpa and that it haunted her to this day. He smiled wryly at her and then admonished her by reassuring her that it was still just a dream and nothing to worry about.

Ali turned and looked out the passenger's window. "That's why I hesitated to tell you about my dream. I knew you would tell me not to worry about it, that it was only a dream."

John, slightly taken aback by her reaction, explained, "I'm sorry, I wasn't trying to make light of your dream, but after all it was..."

She interrupted, "Just a dream. Is that what you're going to say?"

John took his eyes off the road for a second and glanced her way, "Well...uh yes, I guess."

"Well, John, it's not that simple. Every fiber in my body is telling me that something bad is going to happen tonight and the only way to make sure it doesn't' happen is to call it a night." She knew he would be disappointed, maybe even angry. It had been a wonderful evening of holding hands and making serious eye contact, but she knew without a doubt that this was the right thing to do.

John laughed, "Well, I've learned during our time together that when you make up your mind to something, you stick to it. It's disappointing though because we've had such a nice evening. I was hoping we could spend a little more time together, that's all."

She slowly crossed her legs and leaned toward him, "Oh, I know, John. It was a wonderful evening and I'm so sorry to call it short. But I promised my niece that after she and Aunt Ella finish baking cookies, that she could come over to my place for a sleepover."

"No problem, I understand."

Ali scooted closer and laid her hand on his forearm. "I know! Why don't you come in for a minute and meet my Aunt Ella and Gabby. I've told them all about you and I'm sure they would love to meet you."

John shrugged, "Sure."

"Oh thank you, John," Ali was beaming.

"Not so fast, Ali, I do have one condition."

"And what is that?"

"We have to do a Ground Hog day."

Ali knew that John was referring to the Bill Murray movie, "Ground Hog Day", in which he would wake up every morning and have a chance to repeat the day before. "I would love that," she replied. "Ground Hog Day it is."

"Great, then we'll go to dinner next Saturday night, take in a movie, and then go back to my place for a swim. Agreed? "He stuck his hand toward her.

She smiled and clasped both of her hands around his outstretched hand. "Agreed!"

"Super!" he said, as the sleek auto darted through the roundabout and headed south towards Ali's place on Lake Harris.

Chapter 33

There was silence in the car for a few minutes and then Ali spoke up. "John, there's something else I've wanted to talk to you about before we get to Aunt Ella's, if you don't mind."

John smiled and replied, "I hope it's not another dream."

"Oh no, nothing like that. It's just that we've never really had a heart-to-heart talk."

John chuckled nervously, "Oh boy, we're getting a little heavy now."

Ali realized that talking about feelings wasn't easy for most men, especially a man like John. She and John had been dating for a while and she felt it was time for them to open up with each other, even if it made John somewhat uncomfortable.

"Oh no, it's nothing heavy, just some things I

would like to talk to you about."

John turned toward her, "I want you to know that if you are going to propose to me tonight, I'll probably say yes!" He laughed heartily and patted her hand, "Sorry, I just couldn't resist."

"Smarty!"

"I know, please go on, I'm all ears."

"You're so funny. But seriously, I do have some things on my mind."

"Like I said, I'm all ears."

"Well, we've only been dating for a few weeks, but I hope you'll agree that it seems that things are becoming more serious between us as time passes."

John nodded. "Hope so."

"And I think you know by now that I'm a pretty moral person. I know I go to the bars and enjoy having a good time, but when it comes to relationships, I am very much an old fashioned person—a one woman, one man sort of girl."

John interrupted, "Am I seeing anyone else right now. Is that what you were going to ask me?"

Ali's cheeks turned a little pink, "Well...uh yes it is." Her eyes fastened on John waiting for his reply.

John grinned, "And what if I said yes? Would it make a difference? Would you continue to see me?"

Ali turned and leaned back against the seat. She had been thrown off her game by the unexpected answer. She hesitated. For the first time since they had started dating, John had her back on her heels and she wasn't sure what to say. "Uh...I guess that's where I was heading. It's just that you got me there a little sooner than I expected."

John's brow lifted, "And?"

Ali suddenly realized that she had painted herself into a corner. She truly felt that they were at a point in their relationship where he should not be seeing other people. She knew John had feelings for her and she was beginning to feel close to him. In Ali's world, trust and commitment mean everything, even if both are single. She could never commit herself to John emotionally, unless she knew that he was seeing her and only her. But another side of her was afraid that if she told him how she truly felt, he might feel too confined by their relationship and start to look elsewhere for companionship. She swallowed hard and continued, "To be honest, John, it would bother me if you were seeing other women right now."

John shook his head, "Well, to be quite frank, since my divorce, I've been playing the field, avoiding commitment, if you know what I mean."

Ali nodded.

"And then you came along and..." he paused.

"And...?"

"I began to realize there might be more important things in life than one night stands."

"Might be?"

"Don't expect miracles."

"John!"

"Okay, there are definitely more important things in life than one night stands. Happy?"

"Yes."

He grinned, "Now that we have that settled, I want you to know that I think you're special, very, very, special."

Ali beamed, "Ah...that was sweet! Thank you so much, but you still haven't told me, you know...."

"If I'm seeing anyone right now? Well, I was seeing someone when we first started dating, but that's over now. So no, I'm not seeing anyone else right now and I don't intend to."

Ali leaned over and gave him a quick peck on the cheek, causing him to almost go off the road. She giggled, "Good."

A sudden, exaggerated smile, spread across John's face, "Are we all happy now?"

Eyes twinkling, Ali quickly replied. "Yes, yes, we are."

"Great." John turned right and merged into the fast moving traffic on Highway 441 south and headed for Lake Harris.

Chapter 34

The town square at Brownwood was buzzing with activity as Lex rounded the last curve and pulled into an open parking space across from City Fire. He turned off the engine and reached inside his front jeans pocket and pulled out that little plastic bottle. With hands shaking, he dumped several pills in his mouth. He grabbed the pint of whiskey off the passenger's seat, quickly screwed the lid and took a big swing to wash down the pills. Tightening the lid back on the Jim Beam bottle, he tossed it back on the seat and pushed open the driver's side door. Between the swigs of whiskey and the pills, Lex was beginning to feel no pain. Staggering slightly, he carefully made his way across the street toward City Fire.

A bolt of fear shot up his spine when he saw a county sheriff's car roll to a stop at the four-way next to City Fire. He quickly looked away from the squad car and continued walking toward the front door hoping that his unsteady gait would go unnoticed by the cops. Fortunately, he avoided any undue attention. While walking through the outside bar area, he nodded at a few familiar faces and proceeded to the front entrance. Once inside the bar, he breathed a sigh of relief. The friendly greeter approached and escorted him to one of the few empty tables available on this busy Saturday night. It was noisy inside the bar and Lex hoped Rudy would show up soon. Feeling fretful and agitated, he needed someone to talk to, he needed someone to vent on.

A few minutes later, Rudy strolled in and spotted Lex waving at him from the corner of the room. He nodded at the greeter and made his way over to Lex's table. He slid off his Chicago Cubs ball cap and tossed it on the table before sitting down.

"You look like shit!" Rudy bawled.

"I know, asshole, you told me that earlier," Lex shot back. "Where have you been? I've been here twenty minutes."

"I doubt if it's been twenty minutes, but then again, you never could tell time worth a damn. And, for your info, I ran home to put the cash in my safe."

Lex grinned, "You got a nice little chunk there."

"You got more."

Lex wanted to go back at him, but he didn't, he just shook his head and signaled at a nearby waitress.

She came right over.

"Can I help you gentlemen?" she asked.

"I'll have a Bud Light on draft," Rudy replied."

"Jim Beam and water," Lex barked.

Rudy's brow furrowed, he seemed confused. "Since when did you start drinking that shit again? You always drink beer."

Lex frowned, "I drink both."

"Anyway, are you feeling okay? You really don't look very good."

"I know, you keep telling me that. I feel okay, I'm just stressed out."

Rudy tossed him an incredulous glare, "About what? All the money you've been making lately?"

The waitress arrived with their drinks and carefully set them on the table in front of them. "Want to run a tab?' she asked.

"Yes, that's good, and when we're through, just give it to me," Lex offered.

"Will do." The waitress smiled and hurried away.

It was quiet for a few seconds with both men sitting and staring at their drinks. Lex wrapped his hands around his whiskey and water and spoke, breaking the uncomfortable silence. "My ex is still seeing that rich guy in The Villages. I think it may be starting to get serious."

The hard-edged Rudy's eyes softened. He knew that Lex still had feelings for his ex-wife. "Listen, Lex, you and Ali are divorced. You gotta give it up!"

Lex was almost whispering now, "She's so fine, so beautiful; I never realized what I had with her."

Rudy leaned forward, "I know you're still nuts for her, but you've got to let go, man, she's on to bigger and better things."

Lex's eyes locked on Rudy, "Better? He's not better than me just because he's got money! The guy is a sleaze! He's been laying everything he can get his hands on. He's a bad dude!"

"I really don't think Ali could go for a guy like that, but she's a free woman, man, she can do what she wants."

Lex took a gulp of his whisky and water. "She still loves me. I know she does."

Rudy sighed, "And why would you think that?"

"I talked to her in the drugstore the other day and I could tell by the way she looked at me and the way she talked to me that she still loves me. We split up because I couldn't hold a job. She'll take me back, I just have to show her that I can give her a good life, a stable life, that's all."

Rudy rolled his eyes. "Is that what all this Jiffy Lube bullshit is about? You think you can get her back by opening a stupid Jiffy Lube? You're delusional, man, delusional!"

Lex bristled at Rudy's comments, "I'm not opening just one, Rudy, I plan on having a chain of them. I plan on being a rich man someday."

"A rich man? You? I don't think so."

"Maybe it won't work, Rudy, but at least I'm trying. I'm not going to end up some loser running a meth lab for the rest of my life."

Rudy's anger flared, his eyes narrowed, "Is that what you think of me, Lex, that I'm some loser, that all I can do is run a meth lab?"

Lex broke eye contact and looked down at the table. He didn't reply.

Rudy spoke quietly trying to control his rage, "I didn't grow up in a good family like you did, Lex, and maybe I wasn't a big basketball hero or anything, but I'm no loser!"

Lex shook his head, he knew he had really stung Rudy. "That was just a slip of the tongue, man. Just let it go."

Rudy was having no part of Lex's weak attempt at an apology. "You're the loser, Lex. Just look at you. You look like shit. You think a beautiful girl like Ali is going to take you back? You're nuts, Lex. That's what you are, you're fuckin' nuts!"

Anger flashed through Lex, "What have you ever done with your life Rudy? You keep jumping from job to job! Hell, half the time you can't even put food on the table! Your kids must be real proud of you!"

The reference to his children inflamed Rudy. He jumped up, leaned forward and slammed his hands on the table in front of Lex. He spoke angrily, but low enough so the tables around him couldn't hear. "We're both losers, Lex! We're two sorry-ass losers at the bottom of the fuckin' barrel. We're the kind of people who sell poison to poor people so they can feel better for a few minutes, knowing that we're frying their brains for the rest of their fuckin' lives! In all the world, Lex, there's nobody lower than meth pushers, we are the lowest of the low!"

Lex glared at Rudy. He started to say something, but Rudy interrupted. "I'll clean out the lab tomorrow. I'll get a couple of the guys to help me. I don't want to see you again, Lex, never again!" Rudy dug in his pocket and pulled out a wad of cash. He slid a twenty out and threw it on the table. "That should cover my beer!" He angrily snatched his Cubs hat off the table and walked out of the bar.

Lex sat with his hands still wrapped around his drink staring at the twenty dollar bill. He regretted calling Rudy a loser, but the booze and pills were numbing his feelings leaving him incapable of feeling any true compassion. He lifted his drink and finished it. He waved at the waitress and she hurried over.

"Two more?"

"Nah, my friend had to leave, it's just me now." Lex looked toward the bar area and saw an open seat. "I think I'll move over there." He pointed at the empty seat.

"Okay, I'll have the bartender get a Beam and water ready for you at the bar."

Lex stood and lifted the twenty off the table and walked slowly toward the bar, mumbling apologies to the people he bumped into along the way. Feeling little remorse about Rudy, he climbed aboard a vacant barstool and immediately grabbed the Beam. He tilted his head back and downed the potent elixir and then banged the thick glass on the shiny bar.

"Gimme a shot this time!" he barked at the nearby bartender.

The bartender quickly poured him a shot of whiskey. "There ya go, mister."

Lex lifted the shot up to eye level, swished it around a little, and downed it—he felt a burn all the way down to his stomach. He set the empty shot on the shiny bar and glanced out the window at the beautiful town square at Brownwood filled with sixty-somethings dancing and talking. *There's going to be one less of you assholes after tonight!* he thought. A nasty grin broke out on his face as he turned toward the bartender, "One more, buddy, and then I'm outa here!"

Chapter 35

Lex fell back against the leather seat on his Firebird and clumsily slipped his cell phone out of his front pocket. After several misses, he finally hit the recent calls symbol. He tapped Tony Canero's number and stuck the phone next to his ear.

Tony answered. "Hello."

"Tony, it's me L...Lex."

There was some hesitation on the other end, "You sound drunk."

"I'm not drunk, but I need to talk to you."

Tony sounded irritated. "Lex, I've had a long day and I was just getting ready to go to bed. Call me in the morning."

"M...Man, you really have changed. You used to stay up all night on a Saturday night."

"I had a long day at The Villages, remember?

Listen, Lex, I know what you're calling me about and the answer is still no. I told you earlier and I meant what I said. I'm not going to mess with anybody or hurt anybody for you, Lex. I'm not going to do it."

Lex sat staring straight ahead, he was perspiring heavily. "You don't understand, Tony. This rich bastard is trying to ruin my life. We gotta do something."

"No we don't, Lex! I'm not going to do anything to that man!"

"Like I say, Tony, you owe...."

Tony immediately interrupted Lex, "Don't start with that "you owe me" crap again, Lex. We had a business arrangement, you got busted and you didn't rat me out. I appreciate that, but I would have done the same for you. My advice to you is to forget about this rich guy and get your drunken ass home and sober up before you do something stupid!"

"Up yours, Tony."

There was a long pause. "You're a mess, Lex. I'm going to bed."

With that, the phone went dead on the other end. Lex quickly stuffed his phone in his pant pocket and started the car.

* * *

Lex was becoming more and more stoned, his head was spinning. He slowed just before entering the roundabout into Bridgeport at Lake Miona. He reached over and punched the button on the glovebox and watched the door fall open. Groping around inside the glovebox, he finally found what he was looking for—his .45 revolver. He lifted the gun, wrapped in a gray rag and carefully placed it on the passenger side seat. He lifted the rag off the shiny gun and stuffed it back in the glovebox. He laid his hand on the gun, it felt cool. Gripping the gun firmly in his right hand, he move it over next to his thigh. Arriving at the gate to Bridgeport, he punched at the metal button, watched the gate open up and drove in.

Chapter 36

Ned Carpenter and his wife had just arrived home after a long night of Triple Play at a friend's house in The Villages. It was a little after ten and almost bedtime, so his wife had headed to the bedroom to put on her pajamas and get comfortable.

In the meantime, Ned had quickly ducked in their half bath next to the foyer to relieve his swollen bladder of three plus hours of Diet Coke. Stepping out of the small bath he saw two headlights moving slowly past the front of his house. Normally, Ned would pay little attention to someone passing in front of his house at this time on a Saturday night, but with his recent concerns about Lex Higgins, he thought the situation warranted a closer look. He walked over to the dining room window, pulled back the curtains and looked out at the street.

"Oh no," he grumbled. "Honey!" he shouted toward the back of the house. "I think we've got a problem here!"

His wife, still fully dressed, hurried to the front of the house to see what Ned was shouting about. "What is it, dear? What's the matter?"

"That's his car, it just went by."

"Who's car?"

"It's Lex Higgins. He's in the neighborhood and checking out John Cullen's house." Ned quickly turned off the light in the foyer making it almost completely dark at the front part of their house.

"Look, honey, he keeps starting and stopping, like he's drunk or something. Oh my, he just turned off his lights."

"Where is he? What is he doing, Ned?"

"Come over here, Ellen." Ellen stepped over next to Ned. He lifted the curtains a little higher as she bent over to look out the window.

"Look, that's his red Firebird at the end of John's drive, just sitting there with his lights off."

"Oh my! That kid's a mess."

"One good thing, it doesn't look like anybody's home at Cullen's right now."

"I remember us passing John when we were leaving for dinner earlier. He probably had a date with Ali," Ellen offered.

"The way he is acting, he must be on drugs or something. I don't think we can ignore this."

Ned slid his cell out of his pocket and quickly punched his speed dial to the Sheriff's Department. After a couple of rings, a very official sounding voice announced, "Hello, Sheriff's Department."

"Susie? It's Ned Carpenter."

"Hi, Ned. I never thought I would hear from you this late on a Saturday night. I hope you're not having any trouble or anything."

"No, I'm not, but I'm afraid there may be trouble in my neighborhood. Who's the shift manager tonight?"

"Rocky is on tonight."

"Oh, that's great, could you please put him on?" Ned was glad Rocky Sines was on duty tonight. He was an old friend and would take Ned's concerns seriously. Ned put his hand over the phone. "He's moving honey, he's heading down the street toward the house that's for sale. I think he's figured out that John isn't home and is going to wait for him.

"Oh dear!"

After a brief pause, Rocky came on. "Hey, Ned, what's up?"

"Rocky, I think I have a problem here in my neighborhood. One of my neighbors has been dating Lex Higgins' ex and Lex is apparently having a very hard time with it. He's driven through our neighborhood several times recently and is apparently stalking my neighbor. And now tonight, just a few minutes ago, he drove into the neighborhood and stopped with his lights off at the end of my neighbor's driveway."

"That's not good, Ned. What's your neighbor's name?"

"John Cullen."

"Has Lex still got that red Firebird?"

"Yes."

"Is your neighbor home?"

"No, I don't believe so. Hold on, Rocky, he just turned his lights back on and he is turning around."

"Do you think Lex might have a firearm?"

"I wouldn't know for sure, but it wouldn't surprise me."

"What is he doing now?"

"He's driving past John's house very slowly."

Ned could hear chatter in the background. "I've just dispatched a car to your neighborhood, Ned, and I'm putting everyone in the area on alert for a red vintage Firebird. It may take several minutes for someone to get there. None of my cars are in that immediate area right now."

"He's driving past my house now, Rocky, he's leaving the neighborhood. Oh my! I just saw a flash of metal by his right hand as he drove by."

"Probably a gun. I'll get the Community Watch guys on it too, they can tail him until my guys get there. We need to move on this one, Ned! If he comes back or you see anything else, let me know."

"Okay, Rocky, thanks."

Chapter 37

Lex held the gun loosely in his right hand as he cruised toward the exit gate at Bridgeport. Cullen's house was pitch black inside and it was obvious no one was at home. Lex had thought about trying to get in the house and wait for Cullen to arrive home and ambush him, but even in his current state of intoxication, he realized that wasn't a good idea. The house was probably covered with security equipment, ready to go off at the slightest provocation. Besides, in his haste to meet with Rudy earlier in the evening, he left the silencer he had just bought at home. He needed that silencer. His original plan was to knock on the front door and when Cullen came to answer, he would blast him full of lead with his .45 with the silencer attached. But, since there was no one at home, Lex decided to scrap the plan for now and leave the area before anyone noticed him. He would return later with the silencer and finish the job.

Lex had been very worried that Ali might be at Cullen's house when he went to shoot him. So he checked out Ali's Facebook page earlier in the evening to try and find out what she was doing for the evening. Ali loved Facebook and posted almost daily. When he checked out Facebook on his phone, the first image that popped up was a picture of Ali and her niece making cookies at Ali's apartment at around nine forty-five. That was great news for Lex. Now he knew that Ali was at home and not with Cullen. As disoriented and irrational as Lex was, he still loved Ali too much to allow her to see her boyfriend blown to bits. With Ali at home and out of the way, he could now have his own way with Cullen.

The cell call he made earlier to Tony Canero was also part of his plan. Years ago, when he and Tony were cooking meth together, Tony had left a black sock cap in Lex's car and Lex had forgotten to return it. Lex happened to find the cap lying on the floor of his closet next to his boots the other day—it must have fallen down when he grabbed his work gloves off of the closet shelf earlier that day. When he bent over to pick it up, he noticed that Tony's name was sewn inside. Still upset with Canero for not helping him out with Cullen, the name in the hat gave Lex an idea.

He could use the black hat to try and frame Tony

for the murder. He would simply drop the hat at the crime scene in an obvious location. The cops would see it, pick it up, and see Tony's name sewn inside. With Tony's checkered past in New York as a sometimes mob enforcer and with two assaults on his record, it wouldn't take long for him to become a lead suspect. His call to Tony earlier was to check out what he was doing tonight, to see if he would have a good alibi for the evening. Sitting home alone all evening was not a good alibi. Lex had found his scapegoat, he could kill Cullen and let Tony take the rap.

Chapter 38

Driving cautiously, Lex eased off the gas and turned left onto 466A. Afraid that his drug and alcohol induced courage would wane, Lex grabbed the whiskey bottle off the seat and took several more swigs. The bottle was almost empty now. A few miles later, the sign at the Shell Station at the intersection of 25A and 466A came into view. He looked down at his fuel gage to see if he needed to stop and get gas. The needle was quivering around a half tank—plenty of fuel to take him through the evening. He looked back at the fast approaching intersection and then quickly slammed on the brakes. With brakes screeching, his car finally skidded to a stop in the middle of the intersection. In his drunken state he had gone past the stop sign and into the intersection. He glanced in his rearview mirror to see if anyone was behind him and then he backed up until he was safely behind the stop sign.

Behind the stop sign, but sitting cockeyed at the intersection, he smacked himself on the cheek several times to try and sober up. Suddenly, a set of bright headlights beamed into his eyes. Lex shielded his eyes against the bright lights and attempted to focus in on the approaching vehicle. It was a silver Mercedes Roadster —there weren't many silver Mercedes Roadsters in the Leesburg area. He watched as the driver flipped on the left turn signal and turned in front of him. Lex's headlights shone directly on the driver's face. Lex was stunned. *It's him! It's Cullen!* As Cullen swerved to avoid Lex's Firebird, he looked over at Lex and made eye contact. Apparently recognizing Lex, he grinned and shook his head condescendingly.

Cullen's demeaning sneer caused Lex to fly into a fit of rage. Ignoring the red light, he slammed down on the accelerator and did a frightening U-turn in the middle of the intersection. With rubber burning, Lex fought to control the whirling Firebird. Finally, he righted the vehicle and somehow found the west bound lane on 466A. Pedal to the floor, he raced after Cullen. With his senses dulled by pills and booze, he was in no condition for such a race. Holding tightly to the wheel, he leaned right and felt around on the passenger seat for his gun. Finally finding it, he grabbed it firmly in his right hand and opened the driver's side window. Overcome with rage, he was now right on top of Cullen's Mercedes. Without slowing down, he rammed into the rear of the expensive car, sending it reeling off the road and onto the gravelly berm. Fighting his way back onto the road, Cullen hit the accelerator attempting to get away from his unknown assailant. Lex hit the gas also. Soon the two high powered vehicles were racing down the road at more than ninety miles an hour.

Tossing all caution to the wind and screaming vile epithets, Lex switched the gun to his left hand and stuck his hand out of the open window. Taking aim as best he could, he began firing directly at Cullen's car. With his vision blurred and nerves frayed, he tried desperately to steady his shooting hand against the strong headwind. Making no attempt to just scare Cullen, the angry Lex was shooting to kill.

The left side of the Mercedes's rear window began to shatter from the force of the bullets smashing into it. Cullen began weaving from side to side in an effort to avoid the bullets blasting into his car. Lex fought desperately to stay behind Cullen's wavering car. Suddenly, Lex felt his car moving beneath him, he had gone into the grass on the berm of the road. He was starting to lose control of the Firebird. He quickly pulled his gun hand inside and grabbed the steering wheel with both hands. Miraculously, he was able to right the fast moving car and get it back on the right lane. He immediately put his arm back out the window and resumed firing at Cullen.

With the chase now reaching speeds of nearly one hundred miles an hour on the rural roadway, Lex heard a siren and caught a glimpse of flashing lights in his rearview mirror. Shaken by the sudden entry of law enforcement into the chase, Lex began to panic. Up ahead, Cullen, running for his life, had raced through a red light without stopping just before a large pickup truck wandered into the intersection from the south.

With little time to react, Lex slammed on the brakes and began sliding toward the massive pickup. The screeching sound of skidding rubber seared into Lex's brain. Realizing that a horrible crash was about to happen, he yanked his gun hand back inside the car and threw both arms up around his head to protect himself from the coming disaster. He let out a deep, pathetic groan just before smashing full force into the side of the two ton pickup—suddenly everything went black.

Chapter 39

"Look at this candle, Ali. I think it would look great in your family room."

"Hmm...I like it."

"It needs a little greenery around the base. That would really set it off."

"Look over here, Jen, there's some greenery here that might work."

Jen walked over next to Ali. "Nah, I don't think so. It's a little too bluish for your house."

"Yeah, I think you're right." She looked at Jen, "Maybe I'll hold off on getting a candle today. I'm in pretty good shape in the family room right now."

"No problem, you know me, always here to help and I just love this store."

"Me too, Jen. They have such a nice selection and

the prices are so reasonable."

Jen giggled, "Yeah, like you have to worry about money."

Ali looked at her good friend and smiled. "I know, I've been blessed, but it's not about money, you know, at least not with me."

"Yeah, and I'm the Queen of England."

Ali laughed and shook her head, "Doesn't sound like I will ever convince you of that."

Jen gently patted her friend's arm, "I know I kid you a lot, but to tell you the truth, I think you may be one of the very few people in the world who really means that."

Ali laid her hand on Jen's. "And you, girl, are one of the best friends a girl could ever have.

"We're like salt and pepper, you and I, but I love ya, honey."

Ali smiled, "I love you too. And thanks so much for spending your day off with me."

Apparently not wanting the conversation to get too sentimental, Jen fired back, "No problem, as long as you keep buying my lunch, I'll be back."

Ali laughed out loud, "Speaking of lunch, where do you want to go today?"

"How about Arnie's? We could eat out on the veranda."

"Sounds like a winner."

The two old friends slipped out of The Purple Pig and made their way to Ali's golf cart which was parked in one of the slots that surrounded the gazebo at Lake Sumter Landing.

* * *

The outside veranda area at the Arnold Palmer restaurant overlooks a large driving range area where folks from all over The Villages come and try to work the kinks out of their golf game. Nearing the end of their lunch, Jen looked out at the range and snickered, "Oh my, can you see that guy at the end of the driving range? Look how he wiggles his butt before he hits the ball, it's kind of obscene."

Ali turned slightly in her seat to get a better view of the suggestive golfer and blushed. "Oh my, I'll bet he doesn't realize how he looks. Somebody should show him a video of himself."

"That would be pornography, wouldn't it?

Both women began laughing hysterically, much to the discomfort of their nearby lunch partners. After enduring several hard stares from a nearby table, their laughter quickly subsided.

"Oh boy, that was a hoot!" Ali exclaimed, dabbing her eyes with a tissue.

"Sure was."

After a few minutes of small talk, Ali suddenly got quiet, her demeanor changed. The observant Jen quickly picked up on the unexpected mood swing. "Thinking about something?"

"Oh no, not really," Ali smiled and turned her attention back on Jen.

Jen's eyes softened. She seemed concerned. "You know, Ali, since you got married, your life has been nothing short of a fairy tale—you've got a wonderful husband, a beautiful house in the Reserve, and enough money to more or less do whatever you want, whenever you want; but I know you Ali, and I know there is something really bothering you."

Ali's eyes suddenly clouded over. She didn't reply. Her pleading eyes told Jen everything she needed to know.

"You can't just keep holding everything inside of you, Ali, it's not healthy. You need to talk about it."

Ali broke contact with Jen. She looked away from her and toward the open area behind the veranda, tears began slowly trickling down her cheek. All the nearby tables were now empty and they were alone. "Oh, Jen, I've wanted to talk about it so many times, but it's just too painful."

"It's about Lex and the accident, isn't it?"

Ali moved her head up and down slightly. Jen quickly changed seats and scooted up next to Ali and laid her arm gently around her shoulder and pulled her close. She spoke softly, choosing her words carefully, "What happened that night is not your fault, Ali. Lex had a whole lot of issues. You can't blame yourself for the terrible decisions he made. You just can't."

Ali dropped her chin to her chest and began sobbing.

"Listen, honey, Lex was on a mission to kill John that night. He was shooting at him when he crashed into that truck."

Ali winced at the mention of Lex's terrible accident.

Jen shook her head, "I know what you're thinking. You still think that you caused the accident. You think that because you called the evening short, it put John at that intersection at just the right time, and if he hadn't been at that intersection, Lex would still be alive."

"Well, it's true."

"Okay, Miss Beat-Yourself-Up, no matter what! There is some truth to that. But Ned Carpenter told you that Lex had stopped at the end of John's driveway that night and turned off his lights just before they met at that intersection. He was stalking the man, Ali!"

Still teary-eyed, Ali played with the straw in her glass. "Lex still wouldn't have seen John at that intersection if I hadn't called the evening short."

Jen was becoming irritated, "Yes, I know that. What I'm saying is that Lex was on a mission to do harm to John Cullen. If an incident didn't happen there, it would have happened somewhere else. Lex was obsessed with him and wouldn't have stopped until one of them got hurt. The toxicology report said he had extremely high traces of drugs and alcohol in his system. He was a tragedy waiting to happen, and I hate to say this, but thank God he didn't take John with him."

Ali turned her blurry eyes toward Jen, "I know, but I still..."

Jen interrupted, "No! No! You've got me mad now!" Jen doubled her fists and banged them on the table. "Listen to me!

Shocked by the unexpected outburst from her friend, a wide-eyed Ali scanned her friend's face.

"You're a good person, Ali! You're the best person I have ever known! You're a giving, caring person! And I shouldn't tell you this, but when we were kids, I used to get down on my knees next to that stupid little bed of mine and thank God every night for sending someone as wonderful as you into my life. You can't be everything for everyone, Ali! You can't solve everybody's problems! And most of all, you are not responsible for what happened to Lex Higgins! You do the best you can in your life and then you go on! It wasn't your fault! Shit happens, Ali! Shit happens!"

Ali and Jen both looked around and then laughed nervously at the sudden outburst. Ali looked around one more time to be sure there wasn't anyone within earshot, then she placed both of her hands around Jen's free hand caressing it tenderly, "Thank you for caring enough to get mad at me, Jen, and you're right, my life is everything I ever dreamed of. It just that Lex's death has been weighing so heavily on me ever since the funeral. I have so much guilt inside of me wondering what I could have done differently." Ali paused, she looked at Jen with loving eyes. "You know, Jen, you and I are so different..."

Jen interrupted again and sighed, "Completely!"

Ali smiled and continued, "Yes, we are completely different. You are so strong and fearless. I could never be as bold and outspoken as you. I wish I could, but I just can't."

"Are you telling me that you are not going to shout 'shit happens' any time soon?"

Ali laughed, "I probably won't. But my sweet friend, there's nobody in this world who could have said the things you said to me, the way you said them. Nobody cares enough about me to show that much emotion! I know it wasn't easy for you to do and I know you said those things to me because you love me—I know that."

The usually talkative Jen clammed up, her eyes clouded over.

Ali took a deep breath and exhaled slowly, "And I don't know if I'll ever get over Lex's death completely. It was so tragic and we shared so much together, but thanks to you, I feel that the bubble has been burst and I can start to deal with it. You gave me the push I needed to open up and talk about it, to try and put things in perspective."

Jen wiped away a tear and then carefully pushed the lunch tab across the small table in front of Ali. "Here, pay this, it will make you feel better."

Ali laughed heartily, paused and then said in almost a whisper, "I love you, Jen."

"I love you too, babe."

Ali lifted her wrist to check the time. "Oh my, it's almost five and I wanted to do shish-kabob tonight."

The waitress appeared and slid the folder with the bill and Ali's credit card off the table. "I'll be right back, ladies," she hurried off.

"What are the boys up to today?"

"Golf and then poker at Ed's house."

"Sounds like fun. Hey, Ali, do you mind if I make a quick stop at the powder room?"

"Of course not, we have time. I'll go get the cart and pick you up out front."

"Sounds like a plan." Jen scooted her chair back and hurried inside to the ladies room.

Ali settled up with the waitress, gathered her belongings and made her way down the steps to her golf cart parked by the practice range at Palmer. With Jen busy in the powder room, she took the opportunity to pause and reflect for a minute while sitting in her golf cart. The little girl that had wanted nothing more from life than to please her parents and be an honest, moral and good person had finally found the life she had always dreamed of—a loving husband, a beautiful home near her mother, and the financial resources to do and experience things in life that she had never imagined. And even though she was devastated by the tragic death of her first true love, she now felt that with time she would be able to put his death behind her. Her chin dropped to her chest as if by its own momentum. Then she closed her eyes tight and began to pray ever so quietly, "Hold him close Lord and grant him peace."

Ali slowly opened her eyes, wiped away the tears and smiled at the silly golfer they had watched earlier as he gathered up his clubs and walked to his cart. Feeling eternally grateful for all she had been given, Ali looked forward with a humble heart to a bright and beckoning future.

Chapter 40

Ed Trager tossed two quarters in the growing pot, "I'll bump ya' fifty cents." He glanced through the dancing smoke from his cigar and barked, "Tell me, big hitter, where'd you learn how to play golf like that? A seventy-eight at Palmer is no easy trick."

"Ah...Ed, I just got lucky today."

"Yeah, I'm sure! You had an 81 last week at Lopez, so quit the phony baloney modesty crap and tell me your secret."

"There's no secret, I actually learned to play golf when I was a kid. My dad took me out to the local muni course and taught me all the fundamentals—how to grip the club, the proper stance, the importance of keeping your left arm straight and eye on the ball, all that kind of stuff. I took a liking to the game right away and started playing all the time with a couple of friends of mine."

"And where did all this take place?"

"Upstate New York, a little town in upstate New York. They had a deal back then at the local muni course. Kids could pay ten bucks and play all day, as many holes as you liked. A lot of days, my friends and I would play forty-five holes of golf in one day. Then I got a career and didn't have time to play. When I retired, I started playing again. After Ali and I moved to The Villages, I took a few lessons at Sarasota and here we are. And by the way, I'll call your bet, Ed." Two quarters landed on the pot. The other players followed suit, tossing in two quarters. "Let's see 'em," one of the boys challenged.

Ed slowly laid down his hand and spread it on the table, "Full boat, queens over."

The other players grumbled and tossed their cards in the middle of the table. A smiling Ed dragged in the thick pot and began stacking the coins. The player to his left rounded up the cards and began shuffling for the next deal.

"How about Ali?" Ed continued. "How long has she been playing?"

"She started a couple of years ago. She and a friend of hers who moved to The Villages saw all the golfers driving around in their carts and thought it looked like fun. So the two of them took lessons at Palmer and started playing the executive courses."

"She does pretty darn well," Ed offered.

"Yeah, Ali was an outstanding athlete in high school."

"I can believe that." Ed squinted through the self-imposed smoke screen in front of him. "She's quite the looker, my friend, I'll tell ya that." He waved his hand around the table. These old farts have neck problems from goose necking every time she walks by." The other players nodded sheepishly and chortled like a bunch of teenagers.

A bemused Tony grinned and shook his head.

The outspoken Ed watched the cards pile up in front of him. When the last card landed, he lifted the cards and spread them. With his cigar bouncing precariously between his lips as he talked, he continued, "How'd you ever hook up with her anyway? I heard she was head over heels for that banker guy—the one her ex shot at that night. I knew him a little bit, and he's a hell of a lot better looking than you!" Laughter once again erupted around the table.

Tony Canero smiled, his kindly eyes narrowed a little. "Time was when I might have taken offense to that remark, but since I'm a now a refined gentleman living in The Villages, I'm going to let it go."

"Refined, my ass!" Ed chuckled. "And you still haven't told us how you landed such a sweet, lovely thing as Ali."

"I'll take three," Tony said. The dealer tossed him three cards. He swept them up off the table and stuck them in his hand. Then he laid all his cards on the table face down and halted the play. A changed man, the former tough guy spoke in a friendly tone to his golfing buddies, "You're right, Eddie, she was dating John Cullen for a while, but he made a big mistake. He lied to her. He told Ali he wasn't seeing other women. The next thing Ali knew, a couple of her girlfriends saw him leaving various bars late at night with other girls. That was it for Mr. Cullen. She never saw him again after that. I guess he was calling her all the time, texting her and everything, but it didn't do any good. She tells me that his shadow never darkened her door after that."

"And..." Ed retorted.

Tony's eyes widened, "And what?"

"And how did you come into the picture."

"This will take a minute."

"Go ahead, we're all retired, ya know."

Tony leaned back in his chair and watched as the others followed suit. He hesitated briefly, staring down at the table as if collecting his thoughts. After a few seconds, he began to tell his story. "I had met her ex, Lex Higgins, when I first came to Florida from New York. We were both in the car business back then and he invited me to meet him for breakfast in Leesburg. That's when I first met Ali. She stopped by on her way to work to bring Lex his sack lunch for the day and he introduced us. I remembered how pretty and nice she was." A look of peace and contentment spread over Tony's face at just the mention of his lovely Ali. "After that I really didn't see her again until Lex's funeral. She looked so beautiful, I was totally mesmerized."

"I can see why. She is one gorgeous woman, all right," one of the boys chimed in.

Tony continued, "After the funeral I couldn't get her off my mind. I waited a couple of months out of respect to Lex and then called her to see if she would have dinner with me. I really didn't know what to expect."

Ed chuckled, "Yeah, you wouldn't think a young gal like Ali would go out with a pudgy-ass old tough guy from the Big Apple."

One of the guys broke in, "Hey, knock it off, Eddie, Tony's a nice enough looking guy. My wife thinks he's handsome. And, he's got..." he rubbed the tips of his fingers with his thumb. "And you don't! "

Ed laughed.

Tony continued. "To tell you the truth, the difference in our ages doesn't really bother Ali. She's very mature and wise beyond her years. She's really not on the same wave length as guys her own age. Anyway, I got up the nerve to call her and ask her out for dinner and to my great surprise, she said yes."

"How'd the date go?" Ed asked

"We hit it off very well that night, so I asked her out again and she accepted and the rest is history. We dated several months and we got married last July."

"How'd ya end up in The Villages tormenting all of us?" Ed quipped.

"That was easy. Her dream had always been to someday live in The Villages and I had visited here a couple of years ago and fell in love with the place, so here we are.

The other men nodded their approval and quickly picked up their cards, anxious to continue the poker game. It was Tony's play. He fiddled with his chips, looked at his hand and barked, "Gimme two."

Tony shuddered when he picked up his cards and noticed the many scars on his knuckles—mementos of his violent past. Feeling regret, he quickly turned his thoughts back to his lovely Al and how her love and devotion had changed him. Wanting to see her face, he flicked on the screen on his phone. He watched as the screen saver appeared showing Ali smiling broadly and hugging him tightly in the front seat of her golf cart. Tony's eyes clouded over. His life had gone full circle now, ending here in this wonderful place with the most beautiful girl he had ever known at his side.

The ever verbose Eddie glanced over at Tony looking at Ali's image and barked, "Ya really love her, don't ya', big guy?"

Embarrassed, Tony chuckled nervously and quickly darkened the screen on his phone. He paused for a second and replied, "Yes I do, Eddie, more than anything in the world."

Epilogue

After the initial excitement had worn off and the honeymoon period was over, a very happy Ali and Tony settled into their new life together in The Villages. Always ready to help someone in need, Ali spent her days, when she wasn't golfing with Tony, on her many charitable endeavors, which included Habitat for Humanity, Meals on Wheels, and her most passionate charity of all, Operation Shoe Box. Big, tough, handsome Tony continued to mellow out to the point where his golfing buddies eventually penned the name, Marshmallow, on him because of his soft, non-aggressive personality. Friendly, but smart, Tony made several savvy investments in the market and watched as his sizable nest egg from the class action settlement nearly triple in size. Life was indeed good for the Caneros.

Things didn't work out quite as well for John Cullen. Feeling somewhat uncomfortable living so close to Ali and Tony, he eventually retired and sold his houses in Tampa and The Villages and moved to a six thousand square foot mansion on the gulf near Naples. Once in Naples, he spent countless hours perusing the many bars and lounges on 5th Avenue looking for attractive young ladies to take back and ravage at his mansion by the ocean. Unfortunately for John, six months after arriving in Naples, he was charged with, and later indicted for insider trading as a result of some upside down deals he did while President of the First Bank of Tampa. After paying several enormous fines and settling up with a cadre of attorneys, John barely had enough money left to purchase a double-wide mobile home in Punta Gorda. The mobile home was located in a most fittingly named development called Paradise Lost Mobile Home Park. Rumor has it that the now bearded and heavy-set John spends his days wading around in the tall grass looking for lost golf balls at a local course in Punta Gorda and feeding a flock of pigeons who congregate just outside the front door of his broken down mobile home. Life's excesses had caught up with John Cullen.

About the Author

In novel number seven and the third in his "Paradise Series," R B Conroy once again returns to the enchanting environs of The Villages, Florida. With a creative blending of life in The Villages with the blue collar community that surrounds The Villages, R B creates an exciting story of love  and retribution. The resulting clash of societies brings the reader face-to-face with many of the problems facing society today, including: divorce, drug addiction, violence, and infidelity. With a common thread of the inherent goodness running throughout the story, this novel offers up hope in the face of despair.

R B's novels can be found on all the dot.com's, including Amazon and Barnes & Noble. They are also available on Kindle, Nook, and most e-books.

R B Conroy's other novels include:

Devil Rising

Return of the Gun

In My Father's Image

Deadly Game

Evil in Paradise

Dreams of Paradise